Jaimi
Happ

Laramie

MW00939324

Dirty Little Secret

Book #5 in the Heaven Hill Series

By Laramie Briscoe

Copyright © 2014 Laramie Briscoe
Print Edition

All rights reserved. No part of this book may be reproduced, transmitted downloaded, distributed, stored in or introduced into any information storage and retrieval system, in any form or by any means, whether electronic or mechanical, without express permission of the author, except by a reviewer who may quote brief passages for review purposes.

This book is a work of fiction and any resemblance to any person, living or dead, or any events or occurrences, is purely coincidental. The characters and story lines are created from the author's imagination or are used fictitiously. Any trademarks, service marks, product names, or named features are assumed to be the property of their respective owners, and are used only for reference. There is no implied endorsement if any of these terms are used. Except for review purposes, the reproduction of this book in whole or part, electronically or mechanically, constitutes a copyright violation.

Edited by: Lindsay Gray Hopper
Cover Art by: Kari Ayasha, Cover to Cover Designs
Photography by: MHPhotography Stock & Custom Photos
Cover Models: Alexander Cheek & Mandy Hollis
Proofread by: Dawn Bourgeois
Formatting: Paul Salvette, BB eBooks

Dedication

*To the people who work with me on every book…you make
this just as exciting as it was the first time I pressed
"publish". Thank you to Lindsay, Kari, Paul, and the
newer two—Mandy and Dawn. I truly appreciate everything
that you all do to help me.*

Summary

Sister
Lone survivor
Scared, but tough

Christine Stone has lived through a lot since the day she was born. Her older brother left her without a backwards glance, leaving her with parents who wanted to use her to better themselves in their cult-like religious sect.

Days after legally becoming an adult, she's given to an older man for an arranged marriage that will change her life forever. Escape is the only way her life can be saved. When she succeeds and sets out to make a new life for herself, she meets Travis Steele—communications and security officer for the Heaven Hill MC.

Loner
Protector of secrets
Level-headed and steady

Travis Steele has been on the periphery of the Heaven Hill MC for a long time. Quiet, he takes his job seriously. He is the protector of the group, in charge with keeping family and friends safe.

When one meeting with the sister of his friend turns into more, he struggles with where to draw the line. She needs a friend, and Travis prides himself in being what other people need, often sacrificing himself for others. As he discovers the life that Christine has been forced to live, it opens up old wounds, new wounds, and secrets that everyone thought long buried.

Turning a chance meeting into love is hard, especially when everyone has a dirty little secret.

Chapter One

"**W**here the hell does he keep going?"

Jessica looked up from her laptop, her eyebrows drawn together in question as she looked at her two friends, Bianca and Meredith. "Who?"

"Travis," Meredith answered, turning around from the window. She leaned against the counter and folded her arms over her chest. "Every couple of days he leaves here like his motorcycle boots are on fire. He can't get down that drive fast enough, and then he doesn't come back for hours."

"Maybe he's got a woman." Jessica shrugged, turning back to the screen of her laptop.

Bianca snorted. "Leave it to the romance author." That had become the running joke on everything related to love, sex, and secrets. It was all Jessica's fault.

They shared a laugh as Tyler made his way into the kitchen. "What are you ladies cackling at?"

"Jessica seems to think that Travis's got a woman," Meredith grinned up at her husband.

"Oh really?" He grabbed Meredith around the waist and pulled her to him. He leaned against the counter, his big body providing a comfortable perch for his wife. "Why do you say that?"

"He's leaving here every couple of days, and he doesn't come back for a few hours," Jessica explained. "Plus, the other day when he was helping me switch over some of my metadata on my book, I caught a whiff of perfume off him."

Tyler lazily slung his arm around Meredith's neck and leaned back fully against the counter beside them. His long legs braced against the floor, and he cut his eyes at the woman sitting in front of them. "Look, Felicity," the ladies snickered as he used her pseudonym, "not everyone around here escapes with their lover boy every couple of days to have a forbidden tryst in a hotel room."

"Whatever." She blew out a breath. "I'm just saying, he's changed since I came here, and if you're wondering where he's going—my money's on a woman."

Late October in South Central Kentucky was a crapshoot. Sometimes, the lingering heat of summer had a sharp hold on the region. Every once in a while, though, if they were lucky, October brought with it cool mornings and a crisp scent to the air that told all the residents that winter was coming. On this morning, Travis Steele knew that winter was coming. He could feel it in every part of his bones, could smell it rising up from the earth.

He walked across the gravel driveway to where the garages sat. Instead of going through the clubhouse, he took a quick look around, hoping that no one saw him. If someone saw him, then they would ask questions and he would have to lie. Something he had been doing for months already; he already felt like a piece of shit. Lying to his brothers didn't sit well with him, but these were extenuating circumstances and desperate times called for desperate measures. One more glance behind him and he entered the garage, got on his bike, put on his helmet, started it up, and off he went. Gravel flew behind him as he made his way down the drive. The faster he could get off Heaven Hill property, the better he would feel.

Once he was out on Porter Pike, he opened up the throttle, going faster than he normally would. The tension in his body was palpable—the sneaking around, the secrets, they were all beginning to take a toll on him.

Travis drove down Porter Pike, turned right at Louisville Road, and then made his way out onto Highway 526. Pulling into a subdivision, he parked his bike in the driveway of a nondescript house before getting off and walking to the front door. Instead of the normal key lock, there was a number pad. Only he and the occupant of the home knew the code to get in.

"Travis, is that you?"

The cadence of the soft voice could be heard before it could be seen. Christine was still very jumpy when it came to having people in her personal space. That was one of the reasons he never called before he showed up, but he had a set schedule that the two of them had learned to agree on.

"Expecting someone else?" He smiled slightly. It was a joke, a new thing in their relationship. It was only a few days ago that he'd tried joking with her. She had giggled just as softly as she talked, and it was then that he knew he would do whatever it took to make her do it again.

"No." She shook her head, her dark hair falling across her face.

Outside, he could hear children playing up and down the street, but he couldn't see them. Christine kept her blinds closed; she never opened them up, even when he was here with her. For the most part, she seemed scared to let the outside in.

"It's a gorgeous day," he started, wondering what the answer would be this time. Sometimes she said yes to going out in public with him, but more often than not, it was a flat no. She usually didn't go out unless it was to work or to get something she needed for her home. "It's not too cold yet. Would you like to go out on the bike for a few hours?"

In front of her, she clasped her hands, her fingers intertwining. "You think it's okay?"

"We'll head towards Allen County if you want, maybe even cross the border into Tennessee. We won't hit main roads, and we won't see anyone that you don't want to." Travis wanted to spend time with her, as much time with her as he could, especially if it was on the back of his bike.

"Just so long as we don't head towards Franklin," she whispered.

He knew that Simpson County was a no-go for her. It had only been once that he had even suggested they go there, but all it had taken was once. She'd had a panic attack, the likes of which he'd never before seen.

"I promise." He held his hand out to her. He watched as her blue eyes roamed the tattoo that went from his wrist to his forearm and snaked up his bicep. She always looked at it. He wasn't sure why and hadn't yet gotten the guts to ask her. Making a come-on motion with his hand, he finished. "I brought you a bandana. We can cover your face until we get to Allen County, that way you don't have to worry."

The tension that had caused her to stiffen released immediately. She always worried Jagger would see her or *he* would see her. Worse yet, one of the men that worked for *him* would find her. And she wasn't stupid; she knew that those men were everywhere.

Travis wasn't sure yet if those people were a figment of her imagination or if they were real.

A bright smile finally lit up her face, and just like it always did, it knocked the breath right out of him. "You ready?"

Christine nodded, her dark hair falling over her shoulder. It was so different than the hair he had seen her with months ago at *Wet Wanda's*, but then they'd come a long way from those first meetings. Travis had made sure that she didn't have to take her clothes off to make a living. He'd made sure she had a roof over her head, food in her belly, and a dependable car to get her from point A to point B. He'd been responsible for all of it, including calling in favors. Those were favors he had thought long and hard about calling in, but knew at the end of the day, she would be worth it.

"I am," she finally answered, her voice still soft.

"Then let's go."

They walked outside, both getting on his bike. Once he was seated, he handed the bandana back to her and watched behind his shoulder as she put it over the bottom part of her face. Big sunglasses covered the upper part before she put the helmet on. No one would be able to make out who she was, and that was the way they liked it. The secret had to stay just that, until it was allowed to come out.

Chapter Two

Christine wrapped her arms tightly around Travis' waist as they traveled back down Highway 526. It was getting easier for her to be near him, for her to trust him, the more often he came around. He was her savior. It was as pure and simple as that. During those dark days when they had first met, she wasn't sure they would ever be at this place in their relationship, but they were. Hell, she hadn't been sure there would even be a place for him in her life, but he had gently never taken no for an answer.

"You've got to let me help you," he begged. "I can't stand the thought of you taking your clothes off for these men every night. Your brother is one of my best friends; I can't let you keep doing this."

She wanted to believe that there were good people in the world, that not everyone wanted something from her that she couldn't give, but unfortunately that had never been the case in her life. Trusting someone was the hardest thing for her to do, and four weeks into a friendship felt like a very short amount of time. "What kind of job did you say it is?"

"A receptionist and front-counter girl at the Curly-Q in town. They could probably fix your hair," he blurted out.

A smile played at the ends of her lips. Her hair did need help in a bad way. "I'll think about it."

As they came to a stop at the Louisville Road intersection, Travis leaned back. "Left or right? We can get there both ways."

The night he offered her the job had changed everything and had led them to where they were at this moment. Right would take them toward town and the possibility of seeing people she knew…left would take them deeper into Warren County until they would have to turn east. This decision would be important, and it would mark a step in either her recovery or her staying complacent.

"Let's go right," she said just loud enough for him to hear over the sound of the bike.

Travis didn't give her a chance to question whether this was what she really wanted to do or not. As soon as she said right, he lifted his feet off the ground and pointed them in that direction. He could feel the bite of her fingers, even through the leather cut he wore, the closer they got to the interstate and Porter Pike.

Fear rolled up into her throat. "Don't go that way!"

The words were shouted next to his ear, and he made a split decision to go through town. They could take the bypass and then Scottsville Road all the way out to Allen County. "We'll go through town, it's fine." He did his best to reassure her.

Pushing her head against his back, she hid, not wanting to see any of the cars that passed them by. Slow tears made their way down her cheeks, and she again cursed the name of the man that had made her this way.

Travis loved the drive to Scottsville. It was long enough that he could open up the throttle but not necessarily have to worry about going too fast. They pulled into the city limits and passed some home cooking restaurants before going out further into the county. This was one of their favorite things to do together, and they had been doing it once a month for the past few months. Pulling into their first stop, they got off the bike, him helping her with the helmet and taking the bandanna from her face.

"You want some honey today?" he asked as they made their way to the Amish roadside stand. Several dotted the landscape, and they had a set route that they always took. There were a few that had special things that she liked to get, and he always made a point to stop at those. This was the last week the stands would be open, as cold weather would be making its way into the region soon.

"Yes, please," she answered softly, politely, as they made their way up to where the honey sat.

The woman who ran the stand recognized the two of them. "Christy," she called to them, her voice heavily accented. "I have one special for you."

Christine, not used to anyone giving her a nickname or calling her out in a crowd, looked scared for a moment.

"Hey, you're good," Steele told her, casually putting his arm around her shoulders.

"I know, just took me by surprise."

She waited patiently for the girl, who looked to be around the same age as her, as she brought the jar of honey over. "Thank you so much, Naomi!"

"My pleasure, I like to take care of my good customers."

Travis reached into his jeans and pulled out the money for everything they purchased, handing it over to the young girl. "Thanks, Naomi," he smiled to her.

"You come back next season, and I'll have even more for you."

Christine glanced over at Travis. She hated to be presumptuous, but she would love to come back with him, would love to know that next season they would still be taking these rides together.

"We'll be here," he nodded as he grabbed their sack and walked them over to the bike.

"If you have plans, it's okay," Christine told him. "I can find my way out here in my car."

Travis shook his head. "Nope, I got plans with you."

It had been this way since the day he'd picked her up on the side of the road and taken her to the CRISIS house. "You don't have to keep hanging around me, Travis," she told him softly. "You got me a house, a job, a car. I'm not a pet project."

"Never thought you were." He shrugged and got back on the bike.

"Surely to God, there's some other woman you'd rather be hanging around with. One that opens the blinds to her windows, maybe?"

This was the first time she'd brought up any of her nuances, and he would be crazy to let it pass. "Why *do* you do that?"

"'Cause I don't want him to find me." She immediately hugged her arms around her middle to ward off the chill she suddenly felt.

In all the time they'd hung out, he'd never been able to find out who *him* was; he only knew that the man she sometimes referred to had made a huge impact on her life.

"You ever gonna trust me enough to tell me who he is?"

"It's complicated," she whispered. If he knew everything that she was dealing with and what she had dealt with, he would go running. She knew without a doubt that she didn't want that to happen. Whether she'd meant to or not, she had come to count on him, to depend on his steady hand and level head to be there, to prevent her from falling when it all got to be a little too much.

"I'll take that answer for now, Christy, but at some point, I need to know. At some point we're gonna have to tell Jagger."

That thought caused her heart to beat double-time. How would Jagger take what she had decided to do with her life? What would he do when he realized it was him leaving that had put her in a precarious situation?

"Please, just let me do it on my time," she pleaded.

He sighed, that wasn't at all what he wanted to do, but he had learned that with her, he couldn't push. She didn't push back, she flat shut down, and then it would take him weeks to get back the little trust he had managed to get from her. It wasn't worth it to push, but goddamn he wanted to do just that. He was sick of not being completely honest with his bothers. He had to wonder about himself—how it was so easy for him to keep living a lie.

"Whatever you want," he breathed loudly through his nose.

Christine could tell in the rigid way he held his body that he was unhappy with her. She hated that, but now was the time she could protect her brother, now was the time that she actually had some control over the situation, and she didn't want to give that up for anything. There were a million times in her life that she had backed off and let other people tell her what to do. She wasn't doing it again. There was a part of her that didn't want to upset Travis, but there was a bigger part of her that wanted to own the fact that she could upset him.

"It is what I want," she told him.

"Then we'll do it your way, but I want you to realize that every time I lie to him, I'm potentially fucking up my spot in the club. And realize I'm doing that for you."

He didn't turn around as he talked to her, but she heard it just the same. The defeated tone in his voice about killed her, but she knew that this was the time she needed to be selfish, she needed to worry about herself, because if there was one thing that she had learned, no matter how much she wanted to—it was that she couldn't trust anyone but herself. She couldn't count on anyone but herself, and that was just the way life was.

"Where's Steele?" Liam asked as he walked into the clubhouse.

The group all had one look for their pres, all grinning. "According to Felicity over here, he's out with a chick." Tyler pointed at Jessica.

"Would you stop calling me Felicity?" she asked, feigning irritation.

"Why do you think he's got a woman?" Liam asked as he had a seat and checked the time on his phone. It was almost time for the kids to get off the bus, and he knew that he would have at least a few free hours. Mandy and Drew were completely in love with their little sister, Tatum, and he didn't even get to hold his daughter when they were around.

"There are many reasons," Meredith piped up from where she sat next to Tyler.

"Do share. I'm not just asking where he is for my health; I need to see him about some business."

Jessica ignored the chuckle coming from where Tyler sat. "He leaves here every couple of days; his beard trimmed, the soul-patch just so, or even clean shaven. He has on clean clothes, and I've caught whiffs of a feminine scent coming off him. Those things taken separately don't mean a lot, but all together, they're telling me that he's got a woman."

Liam sighed. "I don't even wanna be involved in this. When he gets back, tell him I'm looking for him. I'll be taking a much needed nap if anyone needs me."

"Who's at the shop?" Tyler asked, referring to Walker's Wheels, the club's source of legitimate income.

"Jagger was leaving to go over there right as I came in. Bianca's got to do a sort of Fall Festival or some shit, so he's going to go over there after he closes up the shop. He wanted to be close in case she needed help." Liam couldn't help the sheepish grin that came to his face. The way these guys had changed always amazed him. It didn't make them any less dangerous when they needed to be in his eyes; it made them more dangerous because now they had something to lose.

"Did you get the message that Rooster left on the club's voicemail for you?" Tyler asked, seemingly satisfied with the answer from Liam about the shop.

"I did." He cleared his throat loudly. "That's what I want to talk to Travis about."

None of them said anything, but over the past few months, Rooster's name had been coming up more and more. They all wondered what in the hell was going on, but nobody wanted to ask.

Chapter Three

It was dark when Travis made his way back to the clubhouse, and he wasn't in the best of moods. Being dishonest to the people that cared about him and always had his back was tiring, and it fucking sucked. Thinking he'd gotten somewhere with Christine only to get the feeling he was never going to get anywhere also fucking sucked.

"Liam's lookin' for you." He stopped short, not having seen Tyler on the front steps smoking a cigarette.

Travis cleared his throat and did his best to wipe the scared look off his face. "Is he inside, or do I need to go see him at home?"

Tyler kicked his long leg out in front of him, his voice deep in the dark of the night. If Travis didn't know better, it would sound threatening. "He waited on you a long time."

The Native American was a man of few words, and he always made them count. Travis had purposely ignored two calls from his pres. "I was out of range, and I only saw his calls when I hit Porter Pike. By that time, I figured I'd be here in a few minutes anyway."

Tyler took a long drag off his cigarette and leveled his

gaze on their security officer. "I don't know what's goin' on with you. Some of the ladies seem to think it's a woman that's got you so tore up, but I'm just gonna be honest and lay it out on the line for you."

Travis swallowed hard. He didn't want to know what Tyler had to say to him. He already kind of knew what it was going to be, and he didn't relish being talked down to by anyone, but coming from Tyler, it held even more weight. "Go ahead," he whispered.

"You need to get your shit together. A few months ago, I saw something in you—I saw you starting to step up and be what we need you to be at this clubhouse. You were becoming someone that Liam and I could count on, but especially for the last six weeks or so, you've been disappearing and you've been sneaky. Other people may not have noticed it, but I tend to watch what everybody around here does. I don't want to think you're doin' shit that you shouldn't be doin', but I'm getting a bad-ass feeling about it."

The breath that Travis was trying to inhale caught in his throat. Nobody liked to hear Tyler say he was getting a bad feeling about anything. At that moment, he wanted to stop his VP and tell him everything that was going on, but something kept him from it. He couldn't see betraying Christine. Not yet. She'd asked for his silence, and he couldn't wipe away the progress that he had been able to gain with her. He'd worked too hard for it. It just didn't sit right with him, either, to tell someone else before he told Jagger. He at least owed that to Jagger.

"I do not want to think you're fucking us over," Tyler started again. "We trust you with a lot of things in this club, and you are the person who keeps us safe. Being shady doesn't fuckin' fly with me."

For the first time—ever—Travis was scared of Tyler. Sure, he was a bad-ass motherfucker that struck fear in the hearts of anyone that he went toe to toe with, but that was hardly ever his brothers in the club. He saw now what their enemies saw when they stared down Tyler Blackfoot. "I'm not doing that, not at all."

"Then give me something." The tone of Tyler's voice was pleading.

Travis turned around so that he didn't have to look at his VP. He couldn't stand the look in Tyler's eyes. That was the look he gave when he was about to fuck shit up, and Travis did not want to be on the business end of Tyler's fist. "There is a woman," he admitted.

The breath that Tyler exhaled was huge. That made him feel better, to know there was a reason for the sneaking around. A woman for Steele made everything that was odd fit together like a puzzle. "So what's the deal? Bring her around so we can meet her, and you can quit fuckin' sneaking around."

"It's not that simple. She's got…problems, and I'm doing my best to help her through those."

If there was something that most of this club knew about, it was problems. They excelled at that, and they seemed to take in every individual who had issues. Tyler wracked his brain to figure out why this woman was so different. "Are you not going to bring her around?" he asked, taking another hit from his cigarette.

"I can't, not yet."

"Is she related to one of us?" He threw out the off-handed remark. That was the only reason he could think why Travis would be keeping her such a secret.

"Please trust me. Know that I would never do anything to put the club at risk, know that I would never do anything to truly betray anyone's trust. Just know that I'm having a hard time working things out in my own head right now. I don't need everyone else's opinions on it. I have to decide for myself how far I'm willing to go with this. I just…" He stopped and took a deep breath. "I'm not sure what I'm going to do about any of this. I want this girl to be it. I want her to trust me, and I'm working on that, but I can't get her to trust me if I run to the club and tell them everything about her."

Tyler stuck another cigarette in between his lips and put his lighter up to it before cupping his hand around the flame and letting it ignite to the tobacco. He took a very long drag off of it and looked at Travis, took a good look at him, before shaking his head. "You do what you need to do, but you've got two weeks. In two weeks, you need to figure out just what the fuck you're doing with this girl. We can't have you running off all the time, being incommunicado because you're worried about what she's going to think. You're our first line of defense here, and if your mind is somewhere else, then we aren't safe. You got that?"

The words were thrown down like a gauntlet, and Tyler dared him not to agree. "Got it."

The two of them looked at each other, and it appeared that Tyler wanted to say more, but he held back. "Liam's lookin' for you. He got a message from Rooster earlier, and he needs your help."

They were back to where they had started, only this

time, it wasn't so tense. "Is he in there or at his house?"

"He's on up at the house."

Steele nodded and turned on his heel, going back towards his bike, completely fuming. He hated that Tyler had called him out. He'd told him to stop sneaking around and to be there for the club. That pissed him off; he was always there for the club. He worked his ass off. He sat at that computer, monitoring things for hour upon hour—if anyone needed anything technical done, they came to him. He was expected to fix every cell phone issue, every computer issue, every home alarm issue there was. Then at the shop, he was expected to do all the technical stuff there. If someone needed NOS or they needed to figure out which computer chip was fucked up in a car that fell on him too. God forbid he want something for himself, that he want a little peace and quiet with someone besides the people in the clubhouse for a little while. His life was the club, but it wasn't the only part of it. By the time he drove down the driveway to Liam's, he had calmed down somewhat, but he was still furious.

Stomping up to the front door, he knocked roughly on it, waiting for his president to open it. When he did, Steele felt bad. He held a crying Tatum close to his chest, a burp cloth over his shoulder.

"Sorry, she just spit up on me, and Denise took the twins to the Fall Festival tonight. I'll be right with ya."

In the grand scheme of things, Liam had a hell of a lot more going on than the rest of them, yet he showed up every day. Some days his eyes had huge circles under them, and they could all see the lines of fatigue that wore on his face, but he never complained.

Not like Steele's own dad had done. When the going got tough with a child, he got gone and never returned.

That thought came out of nowhere, and Travis shook his head. It had been years since he had even thought of his own father. He wasn't sure what had brought that up, but he hoped that it went back to whatever hellhole it came from. He wasn't for sure how long he sat in the living room, waiting on Liam to make a reappearance, but it startled him when the other man came back in, this time without a baby.

"Finally got her to sleep," he laughed, running a hand through his hair. "Sometimes she gets pissy when Drew's not here to sing to her."

"He sings?" Steele asked, his eyebrow quirking up. He'd never heard the teenager sing before.

"Not well," Liam laughed again. "But Tatum loves it. She's infatuated with her older brother. If nobody else can get her to calm down, he usually can. It's a good thing he's old enough and man enough that it doesn't bother him."

There was a soft lull in the conversation, and Travis took a moment to admit how far Liam had come. If someone had told him two years ago that this would be his pres' life, he would have bet money that they were wrong. "Tyler said you wanted to see me?"

"Yeah," Liam stood, taking a baby monitor with him. "Let's take this out to the porch in case Denise and the kids come home while we're talking about it. This isn't something I want everyone to know just yet."

Now he was intrigued. Liam was usually very forthcoming in all that he did. He wasn't one to keep secrets, even if it was probably in the best interest of the club to do so. He wasn't a president in the way his father had been president. He felt that if everyone knew exactly what they were facing, then that made them a stronger unit, and Travis thought so too. The fact that Liam was going against what he had previously said to be true worried him.

They each had a seat, Liam sitting across from Travis. "I got some information from Rooster today, and he's coded it. I can't figure it out, but I knew you would."

Rooster. That name was one that Travis hated to hear; it wasn't for the reason that everyone thought either. It wasn't the fact that he was a sheriff's deputy and he could easily put them all in jail if he wanted. Only Liam knew how close Travis and Rooster were, and Liam had kept that secret. He hadn't ever used it to advance his position in anything or force someone to do something that they didn't want to do, but apparently today, he needed to call it in.

"It's been a long time since Rooster and I were close." Travis squirmed. This whole last hour of his life had been complete and utter FUBAR.

"I have a feelin' you're gonna know what this means. He left me a message on the club voicemail about there being a package at the PO Box. When I went to get it, this is what it was."

Liam pulled a packet of papers out from under the couch cushion and opened them up, extracting a piece of paper. The piece of paper was a photograph of a place that Steele recognized. There was a spot on it circled.

"What the hell or where is this?" Liam asked.

"It's where we used to play as kids, and where he's circled is where we used to hide stuff so that our moms couldn't find it."

Liam nodded, stuffing the picture back into the envelope it had come in. Travis watched as he stuffed the papers back under the couch—for someone that was so concerned with safety, Liam sometimes had the most obvious hiding places. "Being his cousin and all, I figured you'd know. We need to get out there and see what he wants us to find."

Did Liam have to go there? Remind him that they were cousins? It wasn't like he was bound to forget anytime soon. They'd kept that secret long enough; he'd hoped they could keep it forever. "Tomorrow morning will be better. It's hard to see out there at night."

"Then we'll get a group together to make the trip."

Steele stood up, looking at his pres. "You gonna tell them?"

"It's up to you whether you want them to know if Rooster's your family or not. I just knew you could help me. That's the only reason I called in the favor."

Steele nodded and made his way out of the house without another word. Some things were better left in the past.

Chapter Four

*H*er heart was pounding as she ran from the house, down the blacktop road. Remnants of the snow that had fallen a few days before still lay in patches. Her bare feet hit them as she raced this way and that, trying not to run in a straight line. The last time she had tried to run, she'd learned that the hard way. The bullet had clipped her shoulder. This time was it, though; she knew that there wouldn't be another chance. She either made it this time, or she wouldn't. Christine knew that if she didn't make it this time, she was dead. Clinton knew the sheriffs in Simpson, Allen, and Warren counties. They could easily cover up her murder—she would be just a Stepford housewife that had grown bored of her older husband. No one would ever believe the truth; they would never know the hell she had lived in for two years.

"Christine," the voice called out from somewhere behind her, taunting in its tone.

She couldn't breathe too loudly; he could hear that, and then he would know where she was. Placing her hand over her mouth, she breathed as deeply as possible, willing her heartbeat to regulate so that she no longer panted. It was hard to do, especially with how scared she was. The fear that engulfed her was all-consuming, but the bitch of it was, she didn't know if she was scared that he would catch her or that she would never get away.

"When I find you, you're going to be very sorry," he threatened.

That was the truth, and she also knew that. Her stomach rolled involuntarily, and she fought back the gag that threatened her throat. His form of sick punishment was one she never wanted to witness again. It was imperative to get away this time. If she didn't, she knew that she would kill herself—she would be done. There was no way she could continue to live in this hellhole anymore. No one should be forced into the servitude her own father had forced her into at eighteen years old. Nothing could make her live this life anymore. Glancing at her watch, she realized that the cattle truck would be coming down the road in a mere minute. It was like clockwork—every Wednesday, even if it snowed. The truck…it always made it. She had watched it for over six months, timed it to the second. A mere sixty seconds and she could be on her way to some other place.

"Goddamn it, where are you!" he yelled at her again, his voice causing unwelcome goose bumps on her arms.

He was close, much closer than was comfortable, but she knew that the cattle truck was less than a minute away. For seconds, she had to hang on. Just had to hang on. Glancing at the second hand on her watch, she saw they were less than twenty seconds out. She strained, waiting to hear the welcome sound of that rambling truck. A moment of panic set in when she didn't hear it. It should be close enough now. She strained again, her heartbeat pounding heavily in her ears. What if this was the one time in over six months it didn't come? What would she do? Five seconds away from having a complete nervous breakdown, she heard it. The whine of the eighteen-wheeler as it made it up the hill. When she saw the headlights, she knew that she was this close to making it. Throwing everything she had into her legs, she escaped from her hiding place and kicked her legs into long strides. Memories of running from her brother, Jagger, when they played as kids willed her faster. Her thighs burned and her feet beat against the pavement; she could feel the skin splitting as she pounded against the hard surface. The minute he saw her, she knew it. She felt it against the nape of her neck, but she was across the road from him, and the truck was about to be between them. She couldn't stumble, she couldn't look back, she had to give it to God and hope that he would save her this one time she asked. Running as fast as she had ever run in her life, she threw herself at the trailer, catching one of the holes that allowed the cattle to breath. Fleetingly, she heard the gunshot in the wind, but she didn't focus on that. She focused on hanging on tight. The metal cut her hands, but she knew that she had to put miles between herself and Clinton. He would have to go more than a mile to get back to the house and get into a truck to come find her. By then, she should be at least twenty minutes ahead of him. She would drop off the truck and decide just where in the hell she was going to go. For the first time in years, she breathed. She was broken, but she wasn't dead.

Christine jerked awake, her chest heaving. It had been a few months since she'd had that dream. Since she had relived the night she left. Sitting up in bed, she turned on the lamp that sat on her bedside table. Uncharacteristic tears streamed down her face. One thing that she wasn't was a crier, and it had been even longer since she had done that. Beside her, her cell phone rang, and she smiled, seeing the name of her only friend.

"Hey," she answered softly.

"You okay? The security system detected that you turned on a lamp, and I checked the video. You look like you're crying. You're never awake this late at night," Travis said to her, quickly, his voice urgent.

She breathed deeply. "I had a bad dream."

"Do I need to come?"

She wanted that more than anything, but there was a part of her that told her she couldn't count on him like this, it wasn't right to ask this of him. They hadn't talked about it in depth, but he knew Jagger, and that was almost too close for her. There was a piece of her soul that longed to see her brother, but there was another piece of her soul that was pissed at him. Pissed that he had left her in the house with their father, knowing how he was. Sometimes the two feelings were interchangeable, and she wasn't sure if she'd ever know which one she actually felt. Christine wasn't sure that she could forgive him yet. There was one thing, though, she knew she wanted. She wanted—no needed—to see Travis Steele, even if that meant that she was counting on him too much. For once in her life, she wanted to be selfish. She wanted the one thing that brought her a feeling of peace and a feeling of safety.

"Christy?" he asked her again, using the nickname he had been testing out on her for the past few weeks.

"Yes," she whispered. "Would you please?"

"You don't even have to ask me twice," he told her. "I'll be there in a few minutes."

"I'll be waiting."

It said something about the man he was, Travis thought, as he made his way back to his dorm room still wearing the boxers he slept in, that he was willing to get out of bed at 2 AM and go console a woman that he hadn't even slept with yet. It also said something about the feelings he had for her, feelings he knew that he shouldn't have. Feelings that he knew would abso-fucking-lutely scare her. Feelings that scared him, if he were being honest.

He hurried back to his dorm and threw some clothes on, rubbing his hands over his face, scrubbing the sleep from his eyes. He was tired, so tired, but he knew that she needed him, and he would do anything for her. In the past few months, he had become so deeply ingrained in her life that he couldn't remember what his life was like before her.

"Fuck," he breathed, throwing on his cut and grabbing a cigarette from his bedside table. Lighting it and inhaling deeply, he let the nicotine rush through his body. It was few and far between that he needed those cancer sticks anymore, but sometimes he needed to feel that rush.

Between the two of them, someone was going to get hurt, and he was pretty fucking sure it was going to be him. "Man up, Steele," he whispered as he swung his dorm room door open and made his way through the clubhouse. When he hit the kitchen that lead to the garages, he cursed again. There stood Jagger, drinking orange juice from the carton.

"You lazy piece of shit, grab a glass," he told the other man, reaching into the cabinet and extracting one before sitting it on the counter.

Jagger gasped, taking the juice down the wrong way, and then coughed, heaving as he tried to push the juice past his throat. "You scared the absolute shit out of me. What the fuck are you doing up?"

"Could ask you the same thing, and why the hell are you here and not at your apartment?"

"The Fall Festival ran over, and it was closer to come out here than go to the apartment. B's exhausted after helping to plan it. I was afraid she'd fall off the bike if we tried to go any further."

Travis nodded. He knew that Bianca worked hard at her job as a teacher—she took it very seriously. "That doesn't explain why you're out here drinking orange juice out of the carton, which I have to tell you, is fucking nasty, dude. Germs and all. Who knows where your mouth's been?"

Jagger let loose with a shit-eating grin, and Travis held his hands up. "Don't wanna hear it."

"Hey you asked why I was out here."

The two stood there in silence. Travis' heart beat heavily against his chest. He wanted to tell Jagger, so badly, about Christine. He knew that Jagger wondered about her, he had let it slip once, while drunk, that he had gone back to his childhood home, but his parents wouldn't see him. They wouldn't tell him where she was, or even acknowledge that either one of them was their child. Steele knew that had to hurt. His family was just as fucked up as the rest, but at least his mom, when he did see her, acknowledged him. "Whatever. Can you tell Liam that I had to go take care of a personal emergency? I'll meet everybody here before we head out to deal with the Rooster situation."

Jagger regarded Travis closely, his young face turning serious. He looked a lot like Christine when he did that. "You know, it must be weird for you now that all of us are in relationships and happy with what we have. If you ever just need to hang out, you know that Layne and I are here, right?"

Awesome, now Jagger was feeling sorry for him.

"I know, man, thanks for the offer." He squeezed Jagger's shoulder. "But this really is something that I need to deal with on my own."

Not wanting to be in the same room anymore, Travis made a mad dash for the door and all but ran into the garages. Tired didn't even begin to cover it as he hopped on his bike. Now the lie he was living was becoming increasingly harder to keep up with. He hoped with everything in him that Christine Stone was worth it, because if not, when this all came crashing down, his life would be over. He'd probably be kicked out of the MC, lose every single friend he had, and live the rest of his life wondering what could have been with her. Never had he been the type of person to put all his eggs in one basket, but he had with her, and while he wasn't regretting it, he was wondering just what in the fuck he'd gotten himself into.

Any person in their right mind would question themselves for getting out of bed at 2 AM and driving to meet a woman that they hadn't even kissed yet. Starting the bike, he sighed and drove down the driveway before hitting Porter Pike and driving the same direction he'd been driving for months. Soon, he would need to demand answers, but right now, he wanted to be what she needed because he desperately wanted her to be what he needed.

Chapter Five

Christine was scared that Travis had changed his mind when, after thirty minutes, he still hadn't showed up at her house. She didn't want to examine too closely why that bothered her or why it scared her, but it did. She got up, pacing the living room until she heard the muted roar of a bike. She would know that sound anywhere, it had become one of her favorites. Running over to the front door, she opened it when she heard him on the front porch.

"Sorry it took me so long," he told her as he made his way into the house. "I got stopped on my way out."

"At this hour?" she asked, disbelief showing on her face.

Travis shrugged. "We kinda keep our own hours at the clubhouse. Just so happened someone was drinking out of the orange juice carton. Drives me fucking nuts. There's glasses there for a reason."

She smiled softly. "Sounds like something Jagger used to do."

He tensed, wondering if he should tell her the truth. This was one of the first times that she had mentioned him voluntarily. Knowing that they wouldn't get past this huge elephant if they didn't acknowledge it, he decided it was best to be honest. "It was Jagger, and he asked me where the fuck I was going."

"Did you tell him?" Two feelings bubbled up in gut at the thought of him telling her brother, fear and relief. She didn't want to examine either one of them.

"Have I broken a promise to you yet?"

Something about him coming here at this time of night, something about him dropping everything just for her, made her look at him differently. He hadn't ever broken a promise to her, and she could tell by looking at him now that it was taking a toll. There were dark circles under his eyes, his face was pulled taut. "You haven't, and I'm beginning to think that's been very selfish of me."

Those were the last words that he expected to come out of her mouth. "You've got a lot going on," he tried to play it off.

"So do you. I don't have the monopoly on bullshit and life crises."

"Wow," he chuckled. "What's going on here?"

She sought the words that she wanted to speak. It took a long time, but finally she found them. "Tonight is the first time that I've ever seen you when your guard isn't up."

"What the fuck is that supposed to mean?" It was hard to hold back the tone of his voice, the lack of sleep was beginning to get to him.

"That I'm always asking for your help but never asking if you need mine."

He couldn't believe what he was hearing from her. For so long she had been scared to speak to him, almost like she couldn't put voice to anything she really thought, and now here she was telling him that maybe he needed her help. "What the fuck happened to you tonight?"

"I had a dream," she told him.

"Must have been some kinda dream."

"It was about the night I left him."

He stilled, completely stopped moving any part of his body. Was she finally ready to tell him who "him" was? Was she finally ready to trust him? "You know you can talk to me about that…right? I want to know who this guy was, who made you so scared you had to go to a shelter for battered and abused women."

"He was a bad man." She took a deep breath.

It was on the tip of Steele's tongue to tell her "no shit", but he refrained. This was the closest she'd ever been to telling him the things that he wanted to know, and he didn't want to ruin it. "How did you meet him? Does Jagger know him?"

"I don't think so," she shook her head. "I don't know where Jagger would have met him, but stranger things have happened, I guess. To tell you the truth, I really don't know. I haven't thought about that in a long time."

She was quiet for so long that he had a seat on the couch and leaned back. He was tired, and he thought maybe if he acted like this wasn't that big of a deal she could open up. He leaned his head back against the cushions and willed his body to relax, closing his eyes at the silence of the room.

"My dad knew him," she finally said. "They had some sort of deal."

His eyes popped open. "Like an arranged marriage?"

"I guess, I never quiet understood it." She shrugged,

pulling her legs up to her chest.

He recognized that as a protective gesture and knew he had to tread lightly. Travis couldn't believe that someone their age would be involved in an arranged marriage. It was so antiquated. "How old was this piece of shit?"

"When we got married, I was a week past eighteen. He was forty-five," she whispered, her eyes downcast as she said the words.

"Are you fucking shitting me?" he asked, his whole body coming up off the couch.

"I wish I was." She swallowed roughly against the lump that had formed in her throat. "I was nothing more than a trophy wife for him. He decided the color of my hair, what I wore, who I hung out with. I could only drive the kind of car he wanted me to, only when he was with me."

"Is that why your hair looked so weird the first time I met you?"

She couldn't help but laugh. Her hair had looked awful. It was in that in-between stage of color because she hadn't been able to afford to get someone to do it correctly. At that time, she had been trying to do it in the small bathroom at the CRISIS house, and it had been a nightmare. "Yeah," she giggled. "It did look weird. Thank God you got me the job at the hair salon; otherwise it might still look like shit."

He leaned back down against the couch again, pulling her with him. Very carefully, he reached over and ran his hand through her hair. He let his fingers linger at the end of the strand. "I like this color on you."

It was one of the first times that he had ever touched her, other than helping her on or off the bike. They weren't ones to give into displays of any type of affection. They had never even hugged one another, but the way he ran his fingers through her hair, she wanted to lean her head against his chest and purr like a kitten. "I do too."

"Is it your natural color?"

She knew that he was thinking about Jagger. His was a dirty-blond, sometimes darker. Hers had always been on the darker side. She often wondered if the two of them were real brother and sister when she was younger. Their looks, as far as hair color and eye color, were polar opposites, but their bone structure was almost identical. It was why Jagger had always been called a pretty-boy. "It's a little bit darker than my natural color, but I've always had darker-colored hair. Jagger, when he was little, had hair so blond that it was white. I can remember once we went to the pool and the chlorine turned it green. My dad was so mad."

He took that little nugget of info that she had given him and put it in his pocket for later. It wasn't like her to share things with him, and he wanted to believe that they were turning a corner, that she was starting to trust him. "Why would your dad be mad? It wasn't like it was the little shit's fault his hair turned colors."

"It was just how dad was." She shrugged. "The littlest thing would set him off, and the two of us would be wondering just what in the hell we did so wrong. That's why I was surprised when you told me that Jagger's in a relationship."

He had accidentally let that slip in one of their conversations. "Jagger isn't anything like I would imagine your dad was. He's a very compassionate guy. He and B, they have a great relationship."

"B?"

"Her name is Bianca, but we all call her B," Travis explained. "Here." He reached into his pocket and pulled out his personal cell phone, the one that had all his pictures and real-name contacts on it. "This is them." He pulled up a picture that had been taken a few weeks prior at one of the family dinners that the club was now known to have on occasion. They were sitting so close together that there was no space between them. They were cheek to cheek, and the smile on both their faces was bright. Jagger's arm was slung around B's shoulders, and he apparently hadn't been able to help touching her, his thumb cupped her chin.

"She's gorgeous," Christine said as she gazed at the picture. "They look happy."

"They are. It took them a little while to get there, but they are. I'm expecting them to run off and get married any day now."

"Really?" she questioned. After the hell their parents had put them through, she couldn't imagine Jagger willingly wanting to tie himself down like that.

"Yeah," Travis nodded. "Your parents might have been asses, but Jagger has some really good committed couples to pull inspiration from. He's grown into a good man."

No thanks to her or their parents was left unsaid. "I'm so glad he's happy."

"He is, but I know he wonders about you." He slipped that tidbit of information in, hoping that she wouldn't shut down on him. It meant a lot to their relationship, and he wanted her to want that relationship as much as he did.

She shook her head, her long hair hitting his arm. "I can't."

"You can."

Inhaling deeply, she looked him in the eye. "Please respect that, right now, I really can't. I might work up to it one day, but I don't want to ruin his happiness."

"You wouldn't be, it would make him even happier."

He could see that this caused her anxiety, that somehow she thought Jagger knowing where she was would ruin everything for him. "Okay, I'll keep your secret for now, but I'm warning you, Christy. I won't keep it forever. I'm telling you, if you don't tell him in the next few weeks, I'm telling him. I can't keep doing this."

The look on his face, the tired eyes, the taut features, told her that he was being completely honest. He couldn't keep living a lie, and if she was honest with herself too, she was sick of being alone. Seeing that picture of Jagger, she wanted nothing more than to be included in that happiness. She might even want that kind of happiness with Travis. "Do you have any more pictures of them?"

"I do," Travis nodded. "Have you ever heard your brother sing?"

She grinned, nodding. "He used to sing me to sleep when I was little. I knew he sang at *Wet Wanda's*, but I was always scared to be scheduled on those days or to stick around. I was afraid I would blow my own cover. I haven't heard it in so long."

He grinned back at her. "Then you're in for a treat." He flipped through a bunch of pictures—some of just Jagger, some of Jagger with other people—and then he opened up the videos on his phone. "Sometimes we have parties, and every once in a while, we'll get Jagger to pull out his guitar and sing for us. He did this the other night." He pulled up the video and pressed play, letting her watch it.

By the time the video ended she was in tears.

"Are those good or bad?"

"Good," she smiled. "He's gotten so much better, and he stared at Bianca the entire time he sang that. He loves her so much."

"He does," Travis agreed.

He shut the phone off and then put it back in his pocket. Out of nowhere, he felt arms around his waist. Christine was hugging him. She was physically touching him someplace other than the back of his bike. This night would go down to be one that he never thought would happen but was so surprised that it had. He wouldn't forget this night for as long as he lived.

Chapter Six

The next morning dawned way too early for Steele, and he knew that he had to bring it. Rooster had brought him in on something that he had absolutely no idea about. He just knew that his cousin had pointed him in the direction of something that maybe the Heaven Hill MC needed to be aware of. He met the guys, just like he promised to do, and took them out deep into Richardsville. Even though he had grown up on these roads, he hated them. They were so curvy, with twists and blind curves that made him nervous. There had to be a reason that Rooster had brought them all the way out there. At one point, they had to pull off to let other people come through the road, even though they were on bikes.

"This shit is crazy," Jagger breathed. "I've lived in this area my entire life and never knew this shit existed."

"This is why the county always took snow days last winter and everybody in town bitched 'cause there was nothing on the roads in Bowling Green. It was slick as snot out here."

"Are we almost there?" Layne asked from where he brought up the rear.

"Yeah, couple more miles ahead," Travis assured them

as they got back on the road.

The group of them came upon a broken-down farmhouse. It was obvious that it had been in disrepair for years. Travis signaled that this was where they needed to be, and they followed his lead, shutting their bikes off and parking them. "Is this Old Man Sullivan's place?" Liam asked as he got off his bike and took a look around.

"It is," Travis nodded. "It was abandoned even back when we used to come out here as kids, but it was ours."

"I think Rooster brought me out here a few times, but the memory is hazy. I think we were doing a little more than playing," Liam grinned. "We might have been drinkin' a few beers and experimenting with some Mary Jane."

They laughed as Travis broke off from the group, trying to get his bearings. "I'm trying to think, it's been a very long time since I've been out here." He turned to the left and right. "Tyler, which way is northwest?"

Looking up at the sun, Tyler pointed in the correct direction. "You're gonna be over that way."

Travis took off until he rounded the house and spotted a large tree. "That's it. What he wants us to find is over there, but it might take me a minute to get to it."

"Go do it. This place gives me the creeps," Jagger said from where he stood. He had his gloves on, as well as his leathers, but he was fidgety.

"You too?" Layne asked. "Almost feels like someone's watching us."

"We're gonna go check it out," Jagger told Tyler and Liam as they stood there with Travis.

"Sounds like a good idea," Tyler agreed. He was also feeling twitchy.

"Wouldn't put it past that damn sheriff to be setting us up," Layne mumbled as they made their way around the house.

Liam grinned. "He is not a fan of Rooster's."

"Not many of us really are," Tyler admitted. "You have a much different relationship with him than the rest of us do, you have to admit that."

Liam sighed. The relationship he had with the sheriff's deputy was different than those he had with any of the other guys. He and Rooster had grown up together, speeding down these back roads on bikes that they'd built themselves. They had been the best of friends until that fateful night that had sent it all crashing down. Liam wasn't willing to relive that night just so he could explain to the guys why they weren't close anymore. Not even Tyler knew. "I will admit that, but that's all I'm gonna admit."

Travis groaned, digging his way through years of built up foliage. Rooster knew he didn't do nature, and this was awful. "I could fucking kill him for putting this shit here."

"Are you even sure it's there? Looks like that piece of earth hasn't been touched in a long time," Tyler called out.

"It has been, just not much, but I swear to you, if some snake comes crawling out of this mess, I'm gone. Travis Steele does not do snakes."

The guys laughed at him, giving him a hard time as he shuddered. "Be a man," Tyler laughed.

"I am, but I do not do snakes."

He leaned forward and snatched up another piece of foliage, pulling it back. "Got it!" There was a large wooden box hidden underneath, and Travis pulled it out, throwing it on the ground. When he opened it, Tyler bumped his back and yelled "snake!" making Travis jump back and scream.

"Fuck you, Blackfoot," he yelled. "I got bit when I was little, and it was a motherfucking traumatizing experience. This shit is not funny."

Liam and Tyler got themselves under control while Travis sat back down to open the box. He pried it open and started pulling out an envelope. Written on the front of it was a note that said to give it to Liam. "Guess this is yours."

Liam was about to open the envelope when Layne and Jagger came running behind the house. "Hey, we got company," Jagger yelled. He'd pulled his bandana back up over his face, so they knew it wasn't friendly.

"Who is it?" Tyler asked as he helped Liam and Travis gather their information—not wanting to leave any of it behind, in case Rooster had more in the box.

"Some sheriff car has driven by here four times. It's not Rooster, but the last time, the guy had his cell phone out. We need to get out of here."

Travis was confused. Rooster had directed them out to this place because it was so far off anyone's radar that they should have been able to be out for weeks before anyone knew. He and Liam exchanged a look. Had Rooster set them up?

They ran to their bikes and fired them up. As they exited the driveway, the sheriff's deputy pulled in behind them and flashed his lights. "We ain't stoppin'," Liam yelled. "I got a bad feelin' about this."

That feeling was reverberating throughout everyone. They took the winding roads as fast as they dared, coming out onto Richardsville Road. This road at least had lines, but it wasn't any less winding. Even though their bikes were smaller than the sheriff's cruiser, it was apparent that whoever was driving had much more experience on the road than they did. Travis knew that they needed help, and he knew just the person that could help them. Being a techy sometimes had its advantages. Siri understood him better than anyone else, and he had a hands-free device in his helmet. "Call Cash."

Cash Montgomery answered on the first ring. "Yeah?"

"You know that NOS system you want for your car? That one you've promised to work off on the weekends at the shop?" Travis yelled.

"Yeah," the younger boy answered.

"I'll give the fucker to you if you can intercept this fucking sheriff on 185."

"It ain't Rooster, is it?"

"Nah, some guy I've never seen before, and he's hell-bent on getting one of us," Travis yelled over the roar of the bike, his heart beating wildly as he went speeds he was not comfortable with.

Cash laughed. "Must be their new asshole. He split up the street race on Louisville Road last night, lost a lot of money thanks to him. Word has it that he's gonna be replacing Rooster. I'll be there in sixty seconds; I was coming out that way anyway."

The two of them hung up, and Travis concentrated on not laying his bike down. They were pushing them hard. These were not race bikes, but Cash had a race car, one that easily won him every street race in this county. At eighteen, he was becoming a local celebrity. As they came upon the intersection that connected Highway 526 to Highway 185, Travis saw Cash's cherry-colored sports car waiting on them. He could even hear the rev of the engine over their bikes. In the mirror of his bike, he saw Cash wait until the group of them passed—including the sheriff—and then he peeled out, leaving smoke in his wake. It was a few seconds later that Cash caught up to them using the oncoming traffic lane, to inject himself in between the sheriff car and the group of MC riders. Normally, Travis would feel bad about doing this, but they had stuck a stolen license plate on the back of Cash's car after his last speeding ticket, and he regularly interchanged them. If the sheriff decided to do something, and that was a big if, they would have a hell of a hard time finding out exactly who and where Cash was.

Cash slammed on his brakes, making the sheriff do the same and giving them a few extra minutes. They took the turn-off at Detour Road and then Cash gunned it, shooting ahead of the sheriff car. It was his decision, who was he going to go after? Was he going to go after any of them? None of them stuck around to find out. They rode straight to the clubhouse. As they all got off their bikes, Liam looked at Travis, breathing heavily.

"Call Cash and make sure he didn't get caught."

"Will do," Travis nodded. "I told him that if he did that we'd take care of that NOS system for him."

"Sounds good." Liam started taking his riding gear off. "Just make sure he made it alright. When you're done, meet us at the table, we need to talk about this." He held the envelope up in his hand.

Since becoming a dad, Liam hadn't exactly gone soft, but Cash was only four years older than Mandy and Drew, and he felt like he had to watch out for him. Especially when he had been doing something to help them.

The call to Cash took a few minutes. Things had worked out fine, which made Travis feel better about calling him. He'd hated to call the guy in; he was young, but fuck could he drive a car. There was no one else that he trusted to help get them out of that situation more than the man who drove the cherry-red sports car. After he hung up, Travis made his way to the table.

"Cash alright?" Liam asked. The guy had come to them a few months ago, wanting an engine put in after he'd blown his street racing. Since then, they had all come to like him and had helped him make his car even better. Some of them even bet on him once in a while—it was usually a given that he was going to win.

"Yeah, he was pulling into his house when I called. He's good."

Liam nodded, happy that had gone well. "Alright, let's see what this shit is and then figure out what the fuck happened with that cop."

Liam opened the envelope and dumped the contents onto the table. He inhaled sharply as he took in the pictures that sat before them. They took him back years, back to a place he didn't really want to go.

"What is that?" Tyler asked, turning the pictures so that he could see them. "Are these a crime scene?"

"They are," Liam answered. "I didn't ever expect to see this again," he breathed out.

"What are these?" Jagger asked as he thumbed through them.

"This is the night that changed mine and Rooster's

lives forever. What the fuck is he doing with these?"

No one could answer that question but the man himself. Liam cursed. He had trusted his old friend, maybe too much. Now he was pissed. He'd finally put this behind him and here this shit was. "Motherfucker," he spat, as he got up and pulled his phone out, punching a number in furiously.

Whoever he called must have answered on the first ring. "Explain this shit now."

Within minutes he'd hung up. "Rooster's on his way."

None of them knew whether that was a good thing or a bad thing.

Chapter Seven

Afternoon around the Square in Bowling Green was different depending on what time of year it was, Christine was learning. In the late summer or early fall, there were usually concerts in the park, or they were setting up for the Saturday "buy local" events. Now that they were moving into the winter months, she noticed that it wasn't as busy throughout the day, and at lunchtime it was downright dead. She never seemed to know what would happen from day to day, but she liked that. Routine had been something that Clinton had thrived on, and while she did like a little bit of routine, there was another part of her that liked to live by the seat of her pants. That part of her was Jagger through and through. The phone rang, and she jumped before shaking her head and picking it up.

"Thank you for calling the Curly-Q, can I help you?"

She always had to bite back a snicker whenever she pronounced the name of the hair shop she now worked at, but she loved this place. She didn't know now what she would do without it. Getting her the job here had been one of the best things that Travis had been able to do for her. She'd never had a job before, besides being a stripper, and this was something that she really enjoyed. There had even been thoughts in her head of maybe attending cosmetology school once she got everything straightened out.

"Hi! Can you tell me if Shelby has any openings for tomorrow afternoon?"

Christine checked the calendar that was labeled in pink. Shelby had been named for the Steel Magnolia's character and pink was also *her* signature color. "She has one at 4:30 PM if that wouldn't be too late."

"No, that's perfect," the voice on the other end said. "I teach, so that'll give me time to run some errands and then be over there."

"And what's your name?"

"Bianca Hawks, but Shelby knows me as B."

Christine almost dropped her pencil as she wrote the name down. What if Jagger came with his girlfriend? Part of her was okay with that, another part was scared to death. "Alright, Bianca, we'll see you tomorrow." Her tone was sugary sweet, over-compensating for the shock, but the other woman didn't pick up on it. Within moments, they hung up.

"Who was that?" Shelby asked as she came out of the back, putting some hair clips on her apron. She also carried a broom and a dustpan to clean up after the client that had just left the shop.

"Bianca Hawks," she said as normally as she could. "She wanted an appointment with you tomorrow."

"I love that girl," Shelby grinned. "And her boyfriend. Holy hell is he a fine piece of ass! He's got that dangerous thing goin' on too, ya know, since he's a member of Heaven Hill."

Christine played dumb, but there was a part of her that

wondered what Shelby would think if she told her that Jagger was her brother. "I've heard that."

"Who am I kidding?" Shelby shook her head. "All those men are fine pieces of ass. But all of them are taken, except for the kinda hot, nerdy one."

"Travis Steele." She could definitely vouch that he was a bit nerdy, but he was hot too. Becoming hotter the more she hung out with him. In fact, they had a lunch date scheduled for today, and she was very excited about it.

"Yeah, that's him." She snapped her fingers. "He's hot in his own way, but he is definitely no Jagger or Tyler."

Christine was kind of offended to hear the other woman talk about Travis like he was a second-class citizen. For the first time—ever—she admitted to herself that he was a good-looking guy. He wasn't huge in a muscular way; he was strong, but had a little meat on his bones. She liked that, along with the fact that he was always doing something different with his facial hair. Sometimes he had a goatee, sometimes he had a soul patch, she had seen him with a full beard, and she had seen him clean-shaven. All ways she liked him, even when he wore those nerdy hipster glasses that she usually hated on men. She still hadn't gotten the nerve to ask him if he really needed them or if he did it for a fashion statement.

"He is hot in his own way. In fact, I think he's hotter, and he's really nice."

She hadn't meant to say those words out loud.

"Have you met him?" Shelby's green eyes were lit up with an enthusiastic need to be nosey. "I've never met them or talked to any of them, but I've always wanted to. Jagger's never come in with B, but he's dropped her off before. I have a cousin who used to be a stripper down at *Wet Wanda's,* and she said they were all polite when they came in, but they were badass if someone got out of line."

"I met Travis once before," she whispered, afraid that even that would be giving the other woman too much info.

Shelby's mouth opened to ask questions, but the bell rang, signaling someone was coming into the shop. Christine whirled around and thanked God that it was a regular, and all talk of the Heaven Hill MC was gone. Pulling her phone out of her pocket, she saw that she had a missed text from Travis.

Sorry, I won't be able to meet you for lunch today, something's come up.

Christine tried not to let the disappointment cover her like a blanket. Just because he cancelled plans one time didn't mean he was getting tired of her. It didn't mean he was getting sick of her indecisiveness and her need to keep secrecy. It didn't mean that at all.

"You wanna tell me what the fuck this is?"

As soon as Rooster had walked into the room, Liam was on the defensive. It had been a while since any of them had seen Liam get as angry as he was now, but they all knew it was coming. There was only so much stress he could take, and all this coupled with a baby that was just now starting to sleep through the night. The last year for him had been stressful, and now he was over it all.

"Calm down," Rooster tried, wincing when Liam slammed his hand down on the table.

"Don't tell me to calm the fuck down! I've got too much goin' on in my life to be dealin' with this bullshit right now. This was supposed to be taken care of years ago. We took the punishment; I did fucking time in juvie. Where in hell is this coming from now? And so help me God, Rooster, if you lie to me, I will kill you."

"Are you threatening an officer of the law?" Rooster glanced pointedly at him, still willing to bring up the fact that a badge stood between their friendship.

"Fuck no, I'm threatenin' Rooster Hancock who turned tail and ran when things got a little too real for him. I'm threatenin' the best friend that I did everything I could to give a better life because I knew his parents gave two fucks about him and mine didn't," Liam finished, his chest heaving with the effort of the words.

There was silence in the room as everyone looked back and forth between the two of them. They had all known something had happened when Liam and Rooster were younger, but no one knew exactly what. Neither one of them had been at all forthcoming, and it had always been a thorn in everyone's side.

Tyler was the first to find his voice. "I think y'all better tell us just what in the hell went down. We can't protect anybody if we don't know the truth."

Rooster opened his mouth, and Tyler stopped him with the look on his face. "From the beginning and don't leave anything out. You do, I'm liable to turn my back while Liam makes good on his promise."

"We were stupid kids," Rooster whispered. "Both of us were dumbasses."

"And we thought that nothing could touch us because

of how young we were," Liam added. "It was a bad situation the whole way around."

Travis was getting sick of them talking around in circles. He had enough of that with Christine. He wanted the straight truth, for once. "Tell us."

The two men exchanged a look, neither one of them wanting to go into what had happened so long ago, but knowing they had to.

"You'd like that wouldn't you?" Rooster turned on him.

"Yeah, we all would. I wanna get this shit over with."

"That's funny." He walked over to where Travis sat and loomed over him. "I was threatened with something having to do with you, cuz."

Now everyone was staring at him, questions in their eyes. What the fuck did he have to do with this?

"I was told you're harboring someone—is that true?"

Christine. He had to be talking about Christine. How the fuck had Rooster found out about her? He'd been careful—maybe too careful. "What the hell are you talking about?"

"My boss pulled me behind closed doors today. He plopped those pictures in my hands along with a container that holds DNA that wasn't tested way back when, and he told me that he needs the woman you're hiding. So let me give it to you straight, I'm gonna need you to hand her over."

Travis stood up, even though he was shorter than the deputy. "I can't hand her over, and I won't."

"Somebody wants her back, and they aren't going to stop until everybody in this room is destroyed. You got that?" His eyes flashed, more pissed than Travis had seen him in a long time.

"What do they have over you?" Travis asked again, looking back and forth between Liam and Rooster.

"It's me." A small voice came from the doorway.

None of them had noticed that the door had opened and that someone was standing there, so involved they had been in throwing accusations back and forth at one another.

"Roni," Rooster warned.

She shook her head. "No, it's time. Maybe it's time I face up to what I did that night. The two of you have been paying for it for years."

No one knew what to say as they watched her walk into the room. Rooster watched her with an interest that they'd never seen him show before. "William talked," he told her softly, hoping the tone of his voice would soften the blow.

"Motherfucker," Liam mumbled under his breath.

He got up fast, flipping the chair in his wake. It was obvious their pres was pissed. In fact, they'd never seen him so mad before. "Ya know," he started, chest heaving. He licked his lips and started again. "I figured he'd tell on me someday about some stupid shit I did in his name, but not his own daughter. After finding out I'm really not his son, that made fuckin' sense, but why would he want to hurt you?"

She shook her head, putting her hands to her mouth. Why, she wasn't sure, maybe to hold back the sob that she wanted to release.

"Because I would never do that to Mandy, I would never do that to Tatum. Drew can handle himself, I see that even now, at his age, but fuck...to do that shit to my daughters? He's lucky he's behind bars because if I could get my hands on him." He turned and punched the wood paneling of the wall, letting out a "fuck" that was guttural.

Rooster spoke softly as he looked at Roni. His gaze gave nothing away, but the words and tone he used said tons. "He knew it would hurt me too. I would have to make a decision. Do I care about your feelings or my position at the sheriff's office? Because I'm tellin' ya now, they send that off for DNA, and you're done, babe."

It was weird for Roni to hear that endearment come from his lips. It had been a very long time since she'd heard it.

"Did he just call her babe?" Tyler asked a wide-eyed Jagger, his eyes equally wide.

"I think he did."

They weren't paying attention to the two of them, though. Rooster was still talking. "You're not takin' the hit for this."

She shook her head, tears welling up in her eyes. "You and Liam already have. It's why the two of you aren't friends anymore. It's why you're wearing a badge and he's wearing a cut."

That was the crux of it, the bitch of everything. Rooster knew that he and Liam had been heading in the same direction; that night had changed three lives, but two drastically. Two had never gotten back to where they had been. "What's done is done, and that's not the point of any of this. The point is, we need to figure out why they want to blackmail my ass and who the fuck Steele's harboring. I'm assuming she's a fugitive."

"She's not a fugitive," he breathed, getting pissed at Rooster for coming back to Christine.

Rooster stalked over to where Travis sat, hovering over him, towering the way he had when they were kids. "Then tell me who the fuck she is."

"I can't." Travis' tone was firm, his face impassive.

"You have to." Rooster was just as firm, just as impassive.

Travis now stood, trying his best to go nose to nose with his cousin, but he was too short to be intimidating. Instead, he did what he'd done when they were younger, he swept the knee.

"Goddammit," Rooster yelled as he went down, grasping his knee. "We aren't kids anymore!"

"No we're not, which means we aren't close. We haven't been for years, but I would expect you to give me the motherfucking benefit of the doubt. If I'm keeping a woman quiet from everybody, don't you think I have a reason for that?"

"What'd she do?" Rooster demanded.

"Fuck you," he answered. In return, he pointed at Roni. "You wanna talk about women? What the fuck did she do?"

Tyler slammed his hands hard on the table. "Stop! Everybody needs to take a step back here. There's a lot of feelings going on in this room. We all need to sit down, take a few minutes, and chill the fuck out."

Liam glanced over at the man he now called his best friend and nodded, even though his cheeks were still red and his blue eyes were blazing.

"We can't help anybody unless we know the secrets the three of you seem to be harboring." Tyler added. It pained him that Liam's secret had been kept from even him.

"Make that four," Layne pointed at Roni, who still stood in the doorway. "I think she has an awful lot to do with this."

She nodded, wiping at tears that were falling profusely from her eyes. The tension was thick, and it was more than she could take.

"C'mere," Liam told her, holding out his arms.

She gratefully collapsed into them and listened as he talked closely to her ear. "We're gonna figure this shit out. He's not gonna hurt either one of us again. He can say whatever the fuck he wants. We both know it's so he can try to get out from behind those bars we have him behind. We can make whatever evidence they think they have disappear. We've done it before," he soothed her, running his hands down her back.

"I thought it was over," she hiccupped against him.

"It is," he assured her.

Rooster laughed sharply. "The fuck it is. Apparently someone with a lot of fucking money wants whoever the hell Steele's harboring, so we need everybody," he looked pointedly at his cousin, "to be fucking honest here."

Tyler couldn't help the grin that showed on his face. "Don't think I've ever heard you drop that many f-bombs, Boss."

"Don't fucking call me Boss. At this point, if anybody saw me comin' out this way, I probably won't have a job when I get back to town. Not to mention I broke no less than twenty regulations gettin' that shit out to Old Man Sullivan's place, but I'll be damned if I let that piece-of-shit William Walker ruin another person's life. Motherfucking damned."

Chapter Eight

"It was the summer we turned sixteen," Rooster started. "We were wild," he pointed to Liam, "and my parents didn't know what to do with me. Up until then, I had done whatever they told me to do, but that summer—it was all about rebellion."

Liam couldn't help the half-grin that spread across his face. "Hell, even old William didn't know what to do with me. We'd both gotten a couple of piece-of-shit bikes out of the scrapyard, and we'd worked the last half of the school year putting them together. They were in good enough shape to run—not to run for a long time, but run, and that's all we needed."

Rooster picked up the sentiment. "We just needed the wind through our hair and the open road in front of us. The open road didn't care what kind of grades we made, what time we came home, who we made out with behind the clubhouse." His eyes sought out Roni and a flash of recognition showed there.

"As much as Rooster's parents didn't want him hangin' out with a boy whose dad was the leader of an MC, my dad didn't want me hangin' out with Rooster. We were like the odd couple, but no one could keep us away from each other. We had places to be, all the time."

Tyler shifted in his seat. "How were your parents?" he asked the deputy.

"Fuckin' strict and hard-handed. I did something wrong, I knew about it for a few days. Get what I mean?"

"I do," Jagger spoke up from where he sat, shifting uncomfortably in his seat.

It was then that Travis wanted to ask him questions. He wanted to know what childhood had been like for Jagger and his sister. Had they been scared? Had they known what love was? Had she gone from one tyrant to another, without so much as a break to live her life? He was pretty sure he knew the answer to that last one, but he would love for someone to give voice to those answers. What he wouldn't give for her to open up to him.

"So the two of us found ourselves hangin' out. We were friends, but it pissed our parents off so much that it was worth it, too, ya know? Plus Roni liked to hang out with us. It was fun, we were kids," Liam continued. The innocence they all still had had been a beautiful thing.

"One night, we were at a party—one we shouldn't have been at," Roni picked up the story. "The people throwing it were a few years older than me. There's no way two sixteen-year-olds should have been there, but these two have always looked older, and everybody loved that they had bikes. It made them cool, and even though Liam was my little brother, being related to him made me cooler too. People always wanted us at their parties—they always hoped some of the members of the club would show up."

All of them could relate. There was always some dick-head that wanted to take a picture with their bikes or a woman who wanted to hop on the back of it. To play out the fantasy of being with one of them for the night, just so they could go home and fuck their husband hard. This wasn't roleplaying for them, though; this was their real-life.

"Liam quickly hooked up with a girl, and Roni and I had been arguing. We'd spent the summer fucking around," Rooster chanced another glance at her.

She smiled softly. "Literally."

That made everybody laugh and eased the tension in the room enough so that they could all lean back against their seats.

He cut his eyes at her and stretched his long legs out in front of him. "Anyway, we had spent the summer together, and that day we'd had a huge argument over something stupid. I can't even remember what it was now, I just know that I thought it was her fault and she thought it was mine. Either way, we weren't speaking, and even that didn't matter. The only thing that mattered was revenge."

She snorted. "No we weren't, and as soon as we'd gotten to the party, he'd found himself a cute little piece of ass, and he'd had her up against a wall faster than I could tell any other guy what my name was."

Looking back, Rooster realized what a mistake that had been. He'd flaunted it and thrown it in her face, made her desperate to one-up him. He hadn't been proud of it then and he was even less proud now. Hindsight was always 20/20, and looking back on that night, his vision was crystal clear.

"I found the first guy I could who seemed the least little bit interested in me, and I threw myself at him, Rooster be damned." She stopped then, composing herself to finish the story. "The guy took me to a room so that we could be alone, and he shut the door. It wasn't until he locked it that I began to get scared. I'd been around men my whole life—with the club, with Liam, with everybody. When he turned around to look at me, I realized I was in deep shit. There was a look in his eye that just wasn't right. I couldn't put my finger on it, but it gave me the chills, and I felt like he was walking over my grave."

Tyler adjusted his seat, moving his legs back and forth; this was coming way too close to home for him, and he was dreading what he absolutely knew was coming next. He threw his head back and blew out a deep breath.

"I immediately tried to duck under his arm and unlock the door, but he was too fast. I beat on it, I screamed, I kicked, but everybody was either drunk or high, and they were ready to have a good time. It was a party, it was loud, and it was raunchy. Fuck, I'm still convinced that most people that heard me thought we were just having rough sex in that room."

Liam looked at her, realizing that she was probably right. That night had been insane. It was the one and only night he'd ever had a threesome—and at sixteen years old. It hadn't been until Rooster came to find him that he'd even known that anything had happened to Roni.

"He picked me up and threw me against the wall. He was a lot bigger than me, and I fought, kicked, scratched, bit, but nothing got him off of me. Finally, I just started reaching for something, anything to hit him with. That's what they always tell women; find something to hit your attacker with. I remembered the elbow, so I clocked him in the jaw with mine, and then I picked up what was on the table next to us. It was heavy and I just meant to knock him out, I really did," she whispered, the tears clogging her throat.

"I know you did," Rooster soothed her from where he sat.

"When I couldn't wake him up," she choked out, "I rolled him over, and there was so much blood, I must have hit him three, maybe four times. I didn't realize it at the time, but I'd hit an artery and he was bleeding out on me. I had no idea what to do." Tears came again. "I knew I had to find Rooster and Liam. I knew that they would know what to do.

"We cleaned her up, sent her on her way, and set the room up," Liam finished. "We made sure that someone walked in on it. We had our stories straight. A stupid fight that had gotten out of control. They offered Rooster a camp for wayward teens that would straighten his ass up, and they offered me juvie. My dad wasn't as well liked as Rooster's family. It put us on the paths that we've taken so far in this life."

Liam said it so matter-of-fact that they almost missed the regret in his voice. What would have happened if their roles had been reversed? Would Liam be a sheriff's deputy now and Rooster be a member of the club?

"I still sometimes, in the back of my head, wish I had been the one sent to juvie," Rooster admitted. He had thought about that a lot in the first few days he had been at the camp, but after realizing no one was going to come and get him and tell him that they had made a mistake, he came to peace with the decision and tried to get his life on the straight and narrow. Now, he could admit that maybe he had been too straight and narrow. There was a piece of him that was aching to get loose, to let go, to lose control. He missed that so fucking much.

"You know that camp wouldn't have done shit for me. I was already bad. It at least gave you direction."

"Direction I'm not gonna have for very much longer. Covering this shit up, it's gonna cost me my job this time." He couldn't decide if he was upset about that. A few years ago and he would have done whatever he could to keep his job, but now, he wondered what would happen if he left it. Where would he go? His whole life and the open road were completely ahead of him.

"You don't have to," Roni said from where she sat. "It's high time I pay for my own mistakes. If they want to run DNA on it and they find out it was me, I'll turn myself in."

"The fuck you will." Rooster pointed at her. "I didn't spend almost two years in that camp so that you can go to jail!"

"And I didn't almost get killed in juvie for you to be paying for this years later," Liam added. "Why the fuck is this coming up now?"

"Someone found out about us covering it up, probably from William. And that brings us back to Travis. They want the woman that you have. Who is she and what does she know? Why are they willing to reopen an almost sixteen-year-old murder case?"

"Can I talk to you, in private?" Travis asked his pres. If anyone would understand why he wanted to keep this a secret, it would be Liam. He had a sister that he had just gone out of his way to protect. He was also scared of what would happen if Jagger found out. It wasn't too hard to imagine how pissed off he would be.

"Tyler comes with me." Liam made it a point to hardly ever make decisions without his right-hand man to help guide him. It was something they had settled on informally, but it had worked to the advantage of the entire club. There was never any one-sided decision made.

Travis drew in a deep breath. Tyler had already warned him once about being shady, and he was afraid that was coming again. At some point, being shady with this group would mean being dead, and that's not what he wanted at all. "Okay," he answered, nodding his head.

"Can I come?" Rooster pointedly asked his cousin.

"No."

"I'm gonna figure out who it is," he taunted. "You can't continue to keep this woman a secret anymore. You've got to let her go."

"You've got to shut the fuck up."

Emotions were running high, and Rooster stood to his full height, hitching his chin up, a look coming to his eyes that hadn't been there since he was a smart-ass teenager. "You wanna make me?"

"I could. I just put your ass down a few minutes ago."

They were walking slowly towards each other. Tyler made a move to stand in between the two of them. "Stop, both of you. Damn, we have serious shit goin' on here." Tyler took the moment to do something that he'd wanted to do for a very long time. He shoved Rooster in the chest, making him scramble to get his ass in the chair that sat behind him.

"Asshole," Rooster mumbled.

"Pig."

Liam grabbed Travis by the elbow. "C'mon we'll take this into the office."

The three of them walked the short distance, none of them speaking. There, however, was a lot of tension in the air. Travis knew that Liam wanted to ask him what the fuck was going on and Tyler wanted to ask him why he was being shady. When they got to the office and the door was shut, that changed.

It had been a while since Liam had exerted authority, but that didn't mean that he couldn't rock it. He leaned against the desk, folding his arms over his chest, and leveled Travis with a glare. His mouth was set in a firm line, and for the first time in a long time, Travis was a little intimidated by his pres. "I want to know what the fuck is goin' on, and I want to know yesterday, so you better talk fast."

Tyler stood next to Liam, offering him silent backup. Travis wasn't fooled by the nonchalant posture Tyler had adopted; he could spring at any moment, and then they'd all be fucked.

"I want you to hear me out," Travis started.

"You might want to hurry this up. My patience runs thin these days."

"Months ago, I met a woman at *Wet Wanda's*. You could tell by looking at her that she didn't belong there. I befriended her, and I've helped her along the way."

"That's all fine." Liam took a deep breath. "But who is she? Why is someone trying to hold this over you?"

He swallowed roughly. This was not going to go well. "She's Jagger's sister."

"No fuckin' way." Tyler came off the desk. "He will tear you apart if he finds that out."

"I know," Travis shushed them. "It's a difficult situation, but I need you to trust that I would never do anything to put the club at risk. I need you to trust that I am the guy I've always been."

"See, that's not exactly true," Liam laughed. "The Travis Steele I know wouldn't have kept this shit to himself. He would have come to his brothers for help."

"The way you came to us for help with Denise?"

He knew as soon as he said the words; they were the wrong words to say. "Don't bring my woman into this shit. You know that her situation isn't this situation."

"It's not, I agree."

"What exactly do you want us to do?" Tyler asked.

"Give me twenty-four hours. I haven't been able to convince Christine to let me tell Jagger about her yet, and I don't know why. She's not real forthcoming."

Tyler's mind was working a hundred miles a minute. "We gotta think about why that is. Is she hiding something?"

"She is; I know that much. She ran away from someone that she only calls 'a bad man'. I haven't been able to get her to tell me who it is yet," Travis admitted. It hurt—to tell the people that he most loved in the world—that he may have given his heart to a woman who wasn't telling him the truth. No matter what he said to other people, there was always that place in the back of his head that wondered if she told him the truth. Was this a scheme? Was she playing him? Before, he'd been content to let it sit, let her come to him, but now his back was against the wall, people were questioning his loyalties. His brothers were questioning his loyalties.

"I think it's time you get some answers," Liam told the other man softly. "There's only so often a man can make a fool of himself. You feel me?"

"I do, and it's not like I want to make a fuckin' fool out of myself. I was just trying to win her trust."

"Sometimes you can't win it," Tyler spoke up. "Sometimes you gotta take it."

"Is that what you did with Meredith?" Travis was interested. He didn't know how to approach this woman in his life anymore.

"I didn't take it. She had been through a lot, but I did explain to her at every turn that I was with her and I understood that she needed time."

Maybe that was where he'd gone wrong. They never really talked; he just assumed she didn't want to. And maybe she didn't, but maybe she needed to. "Twenty-four hours?" he asked them again.

Liam nodded. "That's all you get. After that, I'm putting both Rooster and Jagger onto you. Go out the back, we'll take care of the rest."

Chapter Nine

Waiting until Christine got off work was one of the hardest things that Travis had ever done. He'd given himself a pep talk about what a pussy he was being, how he needed to man up and tell this woman what he needed her to do. He'd told himself he needed to tell her there would be no more of this secrecy, that she was going to be truthful with him. If she couldn't be truthful, he was going to cut her loose. That's what he'd told himself.

As her car pulled into her driveway, the fight almost went out of him. He had never been the one that all the women looked up to, he didn't have the air of authority that Liam had, the dangerous edge that Tyler did, the good looks that got Jagger everything he wanted, or the wounded soul that Layne carried around (as he should) like a badge of honor. Travis had always been plain Pete. Nothing was special about him, except for his mind. Now, he was scared that this woman had used it, not in the way that other people used it, but used it to get to him and possibly hurt the people he cared about.

"Travis?" she questioned as she got out of the car and shouldered her purse. He looked frazzled and haggard. "Is everything alright? You cancelled lunch and it got me nervous."

"Nah." He shook his head, rubbing his hand along his jaw. Today he wore scruff, he was contemplating letting it grow into a goatee. "Everything's not alright. I need to talk to you."

The way he spoke the words made her blood turn cold. It was almost the way Clinton had spoken to her. She didn't like it one bit, and it made her nervous. "What did I do?"

"It's not anything you did." It's what you haven't done, he wanted to add. It's what you've made me do, the person you've turned me into.

"Can we talk out here, or do we need to go inside?" she asked, her voice shaky.

"Inside," the tone of his voice told her not to ask questions.

She fumbled with the lock after they made their way to the door, and she cursed herself. When she'd left Clinton, she had promised herself that she would not allow another man to make her feel this way again. That didn't stop her from letting Travis move her out of the way and put the code in to open the door for them. Immediately, she went to the couch and had a seat, pressing her knees together and putting her purse in her lap. She looked down and refused to meet his eyes.

"Stop," he told her, breathing deeply. "Stop looking like I'm about to give you a beating."

"Isn't that what's going to happen here?" she asked, fear that she hated in her voice.

In this moment, he hated the Heaven Hill MC, he hated Rooster Hancock, and he absolutely hated that he'd been forced to take this position with her. "No, I'm not going to physically hurt you," he told her, disgusted with himself.

"Sometimes words hurt just as much."

It was that small voice, those words spoken, that got to him. "Then you need to be honest with me, as honest as you've ever been with me, because right now I could be in a lot of damn trouble over you."

"What do you mean?" she asked, even though she didn't want to know the answer.

"Somebody wants you back bad. They've threatened the MC over it."

She was quiet, her face a mask of shock. There, let that sink in, he thought. Let her see what kind of position she's put me in. Let her see what kind of mindfuck I have going on over this whole situation. It killed him to be quiet for long moments. Finally he spoke. "Tell me."

"I can't," she whispered.

"You will." His voice left no room for argument. If he wanted to keep the life he built for himself, he was going to have to be tough with her. It was going to be hard on the both of them, but sometimes feelings and the possibility of caring for someone enough to love them wasn't easy. He wasn't ready to tell her these things, but he knew which way he was moving, and he didn't want to give it up.

She shook her head, her dark hair flying around her head. "I can't."

"Either you tell me, so I can figure out how in the fuck to protect you, or I hand you over. What do you think about that? You've tested every piece of me, and I've shown you nothing that you can't trust. I need you to help me now, and if you're not going to, then I have to do what's best for me. This can't be a relationship until you meet me halfway." He tested out the authoritative tone that he'd rarely ever taken with anyone. Fuck, he rarely ever had to. In his cave, he only had to answer to himself—Liam sometimes, but usually just himself. Now that he was being asked to answer to other people, he wasn't sure how well he liked that.

"I think I deserve to be handed over to him for making you be this person for months."

He shook his head this time. "Not what I'm looking for, Christy. You matter; you're worth something to me. I'm being a hard ass because I want you to fight with me, not against me. Don't you see that?"

"I'm worth a status symbol, that's all. I'm the one that got away."

"I don't believe that," he told her.

"Believe whatever the fuck you want," she yelled. For the first time, she yelled. "I am the one that got away. Others tried. When they came back, they were taken into the room, and I never saw them again. I know they were killed, I know they were. There was no way they couldn't have been after the things I heard in that room. We had no voice, none. One by one, we tried to get away, and everyone failed. Everyone but me. Now he wants a second chance. He wants to make sure he keeps his perfect record," she blurted out.

"What do you mean 'all of them'? There was more than just you?" He was finally getting some of the answers that he'd craved so badly for months.

"Yes! Off and on there were up to five at a time."

Now he was even more confused than when he'd started talking to her. In his head, he could hear Tyler telling him to take it. She was offering him a little nugget, he had to take it and run with it. Very carefully, he sat across from her and took her hands in his. "I have done everything I can do for the past few months to protect you. My ability is being tested and it's being compromised. I don't want you to go back to this place; I don't want you to live in fear. I want you to be happy and live the life that I know you can. I want you to live that life with me, but I need to be able to be the man that can make that happen. Help me."

She started to interrupt him, and he put his finger to her lips.

"I know you want that life because you ran. If you were down to being subservient forever, you would have stayed, you wouldn't have run. You got me? You wanted to do something better for yourself, something you probably didn't even know that you needed, but you did. If you had that much courage to run, to leave this place that scared you so badly, why are you so scared to tell me about it? Don't you realize that by not talking about it, you're giving him power? You're hiding from that part of your life, and it's still holding you captive. You talk to me about it…you speak the words. You set it free, Christy. You set that motherfucker free and let it fly like a bird." Great, now he was paraphrasing Lynyrd Skynyrd, but sometimes you had to do what you had to do.

"There's no other way?"

Travis could see her warring inside herself. The question was in her eyes, and she was swaying, coming around to his way of thinking. He was as close as he had ever been to being allowed in. That trust was amazing, he could feel it, he welcomed it. All she had to do was invite him into her thoughts, into her memories, into her life. "There isn't. I wish there was. I don't want to cause you anymore pain, it's the last thing I want to do. Let me be real honest with you, though. If you don't do this, if you don't let me in, Jagger's going to find out in the worst way about you. I know that you want that on your terms, not someone else's. Am I right about that?"

She thought about her brother. He deserved more than to be used in the same game that she was. As long as he didn't know about her, they could use her as a bargaining tool—on anyone that knew about her. If Jagger was going to find out, she wanted for him to find out on her terms, not anyone else's. That would require her letting Travis know about her life; that would mean giving voice to things she'd never given voice to before. Hell, some of it she'd never even thought about once it happened and it was over. There was no time to be scared anymore, there was no time to let fear rule her—it could still be there, but it couldn't rule her. She couldn't let it rule Jagger or Travis.

"Okay." She swallowed to wet her dry throat and licked her cracked lips.

"You good?" he asked, only halfway believing that she had just agreed to tell him what had happened with her. He ran his hand along her back, daring to touch her, knowing that sometimes you just needed the touch of another human being to bring you back from the brink.

"I'm not good, but I'll be honest with you. I warn you, this could take a while."

He sat back against the couch, propping his feet up in a

relaxed manner. He put his hands on his stomach and offered her a small smile. "I got all night. However long it takes you, I got the time."

And she knew that he did. Whatever she needed. He always seemed to have it. He would need it in spades tonight because she had never told her story to anyone, and she wasn't sure she could make it through, but for him, she was willing to try.

Chapter Ten

"Clinton was a very bad man," she started.

Finally, he had a name. Even with just a first name, sometimes he could find out who people were. He was one of the best at what he did, no matter who or what he usually did it for. "In what way?" he asked, even though he had some sort of idea. It seemed like it would help to ask her questions, that way she didn't have to necessarily offer anything.

She appeared to struggle with the answer, even though he had provided the question. "He was mean. You know how some people are just evil? That was him." There had been a glint to his eye, even the first day she'd come to the home. The way he looked at her, it was as if someone was walking on her grave, and at that point, she'd known she was in trouble. She had begged her father not to leave her there, had prayed that Jagger would show up every day, but he never came, and her father never came back either.

"When did you find out?" He was storing all the information in his head, so that he could access it when he needed to.

"The first night I was there," she whispered. "There was another girl who hadn't cooked his dinner just the way he liked. He backhanded her with a cast iron griddle."

"Jesus," he breathed. "Was it still hot?" He couldn't even begin to imagine that pain. He'd been shot before, but even that would probably pale in comparison.

"It was warm, and the way the women reacted, he did it often enough." She shivered involuntarily.

There were a million questions running through Travis' mind. "Who were these other women, and where did they come from?"

She shrugged. "That something I could never figure out, because one by one they vanished until it was just me. After me, he didn't bring any more women into the family. I don't know why, I never asked, because I didn't want him to think that he needed to bring someone else in. I couldn't imagine this happening to another woman. But I watched him." She stopped and took a breath, putting her hair behind her ears. "He looked at me differently than the others, before they were gone. In moments, he would treat me with tenderness, but it was even scarier to me when he did that."

"He was in love with you?" That thought pissed him off. He didn't want any other man having some sort of claim on her.

"I think so," she whispered. "In his own way, I believe he was in love with me. That's why he fought so hard to keep me, that's why it killed him when I went away, why I think he's still trying to find me."

He hated to be the one to break the news to her, that this man *was* still trying to find her and he now had the club up against a wall. "I'm going to be completely honest with you, and because of that, I need you to be completely honest with me."

She still wasn't sure that she could do that, but she nodded anyway.

"He is trying to find you, and he's threatened the club. I'm going to have to tell Jagger about you. I've been given twenty-four hours to get him on board. If not, it's not going to matter. I need you to be honest with me and let us protect you."

She gasped, the color draining from her face. "What?"

"I can't explain everything to you right now, but I need you to trust me when I tell you that he's threatened some very powerful people within the club, and those people are not gonna sit back and let him play them for a fool. They will retaliate. This will be very ugly, and I want to make sure that you're protected. In order to do that, I need you to be honest with me. What was his business? Why did he want you? What did he do to you?"

"I can't." She shook her head, closing her eyes. "I can't tell you all that." It was embarrassing, and she would be relieving moments and memories that she'd sworn she would not go back to ever again. That had been the only thing that had gotten her up in the morning at the CRISIS center, the fact that she had told herself she did not have to relive her captivity. It was beginning to look like he'd even ruined that for her.

"You have to, Christy." His voice took on a hard edge to it. "I'm fixing to tell one of my brothers that I've known this secret for months and haven't told him. Jagger will rip me apart, and damnit, I need to know it's for something." He was desperate. "I've followed you around for months, like a goddamn puppy dog. I've helped you try to get your life back together. I need you to throw me something here."

Before he knew what she was doing, she'd thrown herself at him, circled her arms around his neck and pulled him down to her, capturing his lips with hers. It was as if a bomb had gone off in his body. He had been on edge with her for weeks, but he hadn't wanted to admit it to himself, he was trying to be the good guy for once. His fingers tangled in her hair and pulled, situating it to his liking as he took over the kiss, trailing his other hand down her side, cupping her hip as he gently pushed her down onto the couch. His body covered hers, but he was careful to keep most of his weight off, until she hooked her legs around his waist.

"Travis," she breathed. How had they gotten here? She wasn't sure; she just knew she hadn't wanted to talk to him anymore. She didn't want to think of the things she'd experienced in that house; she wanted to make new memories and erase the bad ones. If her life was going to implode, she wanted one memory of something good happening to her. She pushed against his T-shirt, running her fingers up the skin she had just exposed.

It took a super-human force of will, but he pulled himself back from the out-of-control kiss. "Stop," he breathed heavily against her lips. "Stop."

It was like throwing cold water over her and she felt stupid. "I'm sorry."

"No, don't do that," he told her. "There's nothing to be sorry for, but I can't let you distract me from why I'm here. I still need answers."

"Can I answer them in the morning? I'm really tired,

and I need you to trust me. I need to get my head in the right place," she told him. "I just need some time to myself."

Could he do that? "Promise me that you'll keep the system on, that you won't leave this house. I don't think it's safe."

"I promise," she told him, breathing a sigh of relief.

"Fine, I'll be here first thing in the morning, and then, I want all the answers to every question I have."

She nodded and knew he was telling her the truth. They had come to an impasse in their relationship, and now it was either time for her to run or stay and fight. Honestly, she still wasn't sure what she was going to do.

Steele hadn't been sure he'd made the right decision, leaving Christine at her house by herself. He had the distinct impression that she was going to run. If she did, he would find her, he had her tech'd up. She couldn't even begin to know how many tracking devices she carried on her. He had hoped that she would come back to the clubhouse with him, that she would accept the things he was telling her, but she had to come to grips with it in her own mind, he reasoned. He understood that, but it didn't mean that he had to like it.

Steele groaned and leaned against the soft cushion of the chair that was his throne when he was in the cave. Every time other members of the club came in, they would give him shit about how he sat in a recliner and not a computer chair, but he just brushed it off. Let them sit at a computer for most of their damn day and not be comfortable.

He was on edge after his afternoon and evening with Christine. She was driving him insane. Every day she seemed to accept him more and become more comfortable with his presence, but on the same token, it was killing him. Their kiss this evening played in the forefront of his mind, like a looping movie. He'd never wanted a woman this bad in his life. As a member of the Heaven Hill MC, he usually had his pick of women, although he rarely ever indulged. It just seemed easier that way. When you did indulge, you had women that thought they were going to be wearing your patch the next day, and that wasn't what he wanted. It hadn't ever been what he wanted.

Rolling his head around on his shoulders, he let out a deep breath and glanced at his watch. It was almost time to turn in. First, he had to do his nightly ritual. When he'd wired up security at Christine's house, at her request he had put cameras in different rooms. She was aware that one was in her bedroom. He looked in on her every night before she went to bed. Christine Stone was a creature of habit; every night, no matter if it was weekday or weekend, if she was home, she was in bed at 11 PM. Tonight, when he flipped the switch to see her house and to hone in on that room, he was surprised to see the small bedside lamp on— it was 11:20.

"Shit, I hope she's not fucking running," he muttered as he zoomed in.

What he saw there made him gasp and his eyes widen. Christine's lower body was covered by a thin sheet, which was unusual in and of itself. Normally, even in the heat of summer, she used a thick blanket. Very plainly, he could see her right hand in between her legs while her left hand was at her breast. It made him a bastard, but he got up from his chair and quickly shut the door to his cave. When the door was shut, no one came in, and he knew that he wanted this to be an absolutely private performance.

Getting back over to his chair, he groaned loudly. The sheet was now gone from her lower body, kicked off by the scissoring of her thighs. It wasn't indecent, she was still fully clothed, but he could see her hand working her core under her lacy underwear, and the hand at her breast now worked her nipple that was hard against the fabric of her T-shirt. Steele knew he should look away, but she was so goddamn gorgeous, so uninhibited, he couldn't.

Her head had fallen back against the pillow, exposing the length of her neck, making him wish he were there to drop kisses along that column. Maybe nip his teeth along the smooth skin that he knew was there. He'd been close to her enough times to know just how smooth that skin was.

"C'mon, baby," he mumbled as he turned the sound on for that camera. Immediately, he could hear the soft panting of her breath.

Her mouth now hung open and her chest heaved. The fingers at her core had picked up speed, and now she lifted herself off the bed in a rhythm almost as if she was imagining them together in bed.

Steele's clothes felt tight against his body as he watched her dig her heels into the mattress. As he watched the hand that had been at her breast move down to the hem of her shirt, he sat entranced as she lifted it up, revealing her naked breast.

"Ohhh," she moaned with what sounded like frustration. It was obvious that she needed a little more. He wanted to be there to give her more.

"Don't stop," he encouraged her; even though he knew she couldn't hear him. He felt like an asshole of the worst kind, but there was absolutely no way he could look away. She knew that he had the ability to see her at any time, and after the frustration of the afternoon, he had to wonder if this was her way of inviting him in. If this was her telling him that she was going to be there when he came back in the morning. He hoped to hell it was. For the first time in a very long time, he threw up a silent prayer.

She tugged firmly at her nipple, gripping it hard, before bringing her finger up to her mouth. He could see her pink tongue snake out, wetting the tip, before bringing it back down to soothe the abused piece of flesh.

His tongue snaked out of its own accord, moistening his bottom lip. How he wanted that to be his tongue on her flesh, his fingers inside her, his body covering her. He was entranced as he watched—a light sheen of sweat could be seen coating her chest as she arched her back, shoving her head harder back against the pillow. Her dark hair was stark against the white pillowcase, and it made him want to bury his hands in her hair, to take control of her pleasure, the way he'd tried to that afternoon.

At his desk, Travis put his hands out, gripping the hard wood, his body tight with tension. He wanted her to get there almost as badly as if he was the one driving her body to orgasm. "Let it go," he whispered, as he watched a bead of sweat roll down her neck.

It was almost like she heard him. The panting reached a

fevered pitch and her mouth opened wide. Harsh breaths, choppy in their cadence, escaped before she took the hand off her breast and covered her mouth with it. Her scream was muffled, but her eyes looked directly into the camera. When she was done, she licked her lips and blew out a deep breath. It was then that he not only heard, but saw, the name Travis on her lips. Within seconds, she'd reached over and turned the light off.

"Damn," he breathed, sagging against the chair he sat in. This woman was going to be the absolute death of him.

Chapter Eleven

T he thought of running had crossed Christine's mind many times the night before, especially after she had put on her show for Travis, but something happened in the early hours of the morning. She wondered when it would stop. When would she be able to stop running? When would she ever be able to have a normal life again? It was at her fingertips right now, and she knew that. What would it help anyone if she just gave up? Why did she fight so hard to leave if she was going to live the rest of her life in fear?

It was 5 AM when she texted Travis and let him know that he could come get her. The best place for her to be was obviously at the Heaven Hill clubhouse, even if that meant seeing Jagger again. She hated that she was going to spring this on him, that she wasn't going to be able to ease him into it, but perhaps that was for the best. Especially, if like everyone said, he thought her dead. Hell, he might not even recognize her now; after everything that had happened, sometimes she almost didn't recognize herself.

An hour after she sent Travis the text, she was still sitting on her couch, worrying that she had made the wrong decision, when she heard the rumble of a vehicle pull into her driveway. She could hear the code being punched in, and she knew that it was Travis. The thought caused her heart to skip a beat. Was this going to be awkward after what she had done in front of him the night before?

"You sure you want to do this?" he asked, coming into the house and shutting the door. He avoided looking her in the face, but his gaze swept over her body.

"I am." She nodded; she couldn't help the blush that reddened her face.

His dark eyes regarded her. He looked for the doubt and fear he had seen there so many times before. Now, though, it was gone, and he was happy for that, happy that she seemed to have, somehow, made up her mind on her own. He had felt awful, backing her into a wall, but in essence Rooster had backed Heaven Hill into a wall, and there was nothing that the group of them could do without each other.

"Then I brought a truck, so that we could bring your stuff to the clubhouse."

"Okay." She walked over to where she'd packed her suitcases. Everything else had come with the house. The only thing she needed was her car, and they had both known that her clothes and knickknacks wouldn't fit in there.

"Jagger's not there," he answered the question that was in her eyes. "He and B have an apartment. More often than not, he sleeps there. He slept there last night, and he has first shift at *Walker's Wheels* this morning, so unless someone blows the whistle on us, you won't have to see him until at least tonight.

That made her feel a little better. "I know this is something I'm going to have to deal with."

"You're also going to need to officially tell us the truth about Clinton Herrington."

She started at the name.

"It's what I do, babe. I don't need a lot to go on. I can figure out pretty much anything about anyone if I just have a little bit of information."

"Did you find out anything about me?" she asked softly.

"I want you to tell me everything about you." He tentatively reached up and moved her hair behind her ear. "I want you to offer it, I don't want to go behind your back and find out shit. That's no way for either of us to build trust."

She knew that he was right, and while his hands on her face made her heart kick up a beat, it also felt good. It felt right. Unlike how she had felt when Clinton would touch her. "Thank you."

He leaned in and kissed her on the cheek. "My pleasure. Now let's get your stuff and get the fuck outta here. We need to find out exactly who wants you back."

"I'm sure it's him," she told Travis, her eyes watering.

"It might be and it might not be. Either way, nobody is going to get you while I'm on watch." The promise was in his voice, and they both hoped that he would be able to keep it. "By the way, thanks for the show last night. I didn't get much sleep, if you were wondering."

It felt weird to be following Travis as he drove a truck. They were going further out into Warren County than she had ever been. The turn-off they took at Porter Pike was one that she had always avoided—actively avoided at that. It made her sick to her stomach as they got further out the country road. Her hands were sweaty against the steering wheel, but she refused to let go. She could see him check back to make sure she was still with him every few miles. It made her feel better, even as it made her nervous.

They got to a gravel driveway, and Travis signaled that they would be turning into it. She did the same. It was with great care he took her down the drive, going slow so as not to throw up dust on the hood of her car. As they rounded a bend, what she assumed was the clubhouse came into view. He stopped the truck in front of where two women stood and got out, waiting for her to put her car in park, turn the engine off, and follow suit.

"Is this where you've been at all hours of the night?" one of them teased Travis.

"Jess, not right now," he laughed uneasily, thinking about the night before.

The other woman who stood next to the one he'd called Jess stepped forward and held her hand out. "Hi, I'm Meredith. Welcome to the Heaven Hill clubhouse."

Christine was grateful for a friendly face. She grasped the woman's hand and shook slowly. "Nice to meet you."

It was then that their eyes caught and Christine could see something there. A kinship, maybe, but she wasn't sure. "Thank you for having me."

"I don't think Steele here would have it any other way." She threw a wink at the guy who stood with his hand protectively on Christine's back.

"Okay, enough of this. If you ladies want to stand around and gawk, at least grab a damn box. Otherwise, I'll put out a mass text that says the women around here are feeling neglected by their men and need to be taken care of."

"Dammit, Travis," Jessica pouted. "I'm just havin' a good time."

It didn't escape him that in the time Jess had been around them, she had adopted some of their dialect.

"Give us just a few hours to get her set up and get some business taken care of. Then I promise you can totally do your best to corrupt her."

That seemed to pacify the redhead, and she grinned over at the two of them. "I'm Jessica Shea…I date Layne. If there's anything you need, please let me know."

Travis had shooed them off before she could answer. "Sorry, they mean well, but they can be a little overwhelming—and I don't want them to send a message to B just yet. I had to block texts on their phones for the morning. Do you know how difficult it's been for me to play dumb when they come bitchin' that their phones aren't working? Those two can spot a bullshitter at fifteen paces. And honestly, who texts that much first thing in the morning?"

A grin tilted up on the side of her face. "That's really sweet that you would that for me."

"I want you to be comfortable here."

She didn't know how to react to that, nobody had wanted her to be comfortable in such a long time. Nobody had cared for what she thought in such a long time, that it shocked her. "Thank you."

"No big deal." He shrugged. "But let's go get you settled; otherwise, we might not have any more alone time as soon as everybody else realizes that you're here."

That was exactly what worried her. Would everyone else be able to leave it alone or would they press and pull her in different directions? She knew one thing; she would have to remember to be true to herself here. If not, who Christine Stone really was would get lost again, and she didn't want that to happen, especially when she was just starting to find her.

"Is it okay if I put my stuff on the left side of the sink in here?" she asked an hour later. They had spent time putting her clothes up, and now they were moving on to her knickknacks and toiletries.

"Wherever you want to put it is fine. I don't really have a set spot."

And that had been the truth. It was one of the reasons that Meredith and Jessica were giving him such a hard time. He'd woken them up at 5 AM when he'd gotten the text from her, begging them to help him clean up his room. It had been a mess, considering he spent most of his time in the cave. It had been almost embarrassing. In return for helping him, the two ladies figured they could also be all up in his business.

"It smells good in here, lemony."

Thank you, Pine-Sol. "I like to be clean," he told her.

She smiled from where she was. She knew that was probably a hell of a lie. A few minutes ago, she'd opened up what he told her was a storage closet that he never used and that she shouldn't…an avalanche had almost fallen on her head. It looked like everything that had possibly been on the floor had been shoved into that closet.

"I see that."

For some reason he felt like he hadn't fooled her. "You know don't you?"

"That you probably shoved all your shit into that closet when I texted you this morning?"

He laughed, a blush working its way up his cheeks. "Am I that transparent?"

"Not really." She laughed along with him. "I've been known to do the same thing every once in a while."

They stood in silence for a moment, neither one sure of what to say. "So," she asked. "Who will I be meeting and when?"

"I'm waiting for Liam, the pres, to tell me when he wants to meet with you. His sister is being used as a pawn, just like you."

She hated that. "I'm sorry."

"This isn't your fault. It's the fault of a sick man who found out a secret from another sick man. We need to know what we're dealing with here, and you are our ticket to that. You're invaluable right now, I hope you realize that."

"I'm not sure how invaluable you'll see me once I'm done. Who's to say your pres won't kill me once he gets the info out of me that he needs." She shuddered at the thought, but wondered if she didn't deserve to meet the business end of a gun. Because her life had been so fucked up, she was fucking up other people's.

"He won't. He's a dad, and once you tell him exactly what happened, he's going to be pissed, but not at you. He's going to be pissed for you. He has daddy issues just like you seem to have…the person I'm most worried about is Jagger."

Those were her exact thoughts. She didn't want him to think that he had caused this for her. But neither one of them, when it came down to it, could really deny that. Her brother leaving had amplified their father's moods, and when Jagger was no longer around to deflect him, he'd turned on her. If she could keep that quiet, she wanted to. There was no reason that Jagger had to be miserable now because she had been then. She hoped they could start over and get to know one another again, but before they did that, she had to figure out a way to tell him everything. She had worked on forgiving him for a long time. She was closer now than she had ever been, but she hoped that he would be able to forgive himself.

Travis' cell went off, and he fished it out of his pocket, grimacing before he put it back in. "It's Liam and he wants us up to the house." He rolled his head around on his shoulders, stretching his neck out before he reached into his other pocket and pulled out a pack of cigarettes. "You want one?" He offered the pack to her.

She'd never smoked a day in her life, but it felt like she needed something to calm her nerves, her heart beat like it would come out of her chest. "Sure."

"Have you ever smoked a cigarette before?" he asked, a small smile playing on his face.

"Well, no, but I gotta do something to calm down."

He pulled a fresh cigarette out of his pack and put the

filtered end up to his mouth. She watched as he lit it, cupping his hand around the flame and the burning tip. He inhaled deeply and then blew the smoke away from her face. Steele licked his lips and held it up to her. "Here ya go."

She eyed him, not sure how she felt about taking it from him. It seemed like something a couple would do, and that wasn't officially what they were, but there was another part of her that loved the fact her lips were about to touch where his just had. It was that desire that won out. Christine grabbed the cigarette from his fingers and stuck it in her mouth, inhaling like she'd seen people in the movies and in real-life do on occasion.

"Not too deep," he cautioned as she started coughing loudly. "How is it?" he asked, a grin on his face.

"Great," she wheezed. "Absolutely great."

Chapter Twelve

"So this is the infamous Christine Stone?"

Christine did her best not to be intimidated by the man who stood before her, but authority oozed off of him in waves. He wore it like a badge of honor—it almost reminded her of Clinton.

"This is her." The don't-be-a-dick tone of Travis' voice told Liam that maybe he had laid it on a little too thick, but they were all on edge. Someone was threatening the club and members of their family.

"Why don't you have a seat?" he asked, sitting at his kitchen table.

She did so, breathing a sigh of relief when Travis sat down beside her. She was half afraid that Liam would say he couldn't be a part of what was starting to feel very much like an interrogation.

"I'm not trying to scare you, honestly I'm not," Liam started, as he reached over and pulled a cigarette out of a pack that sat on the table. "You want one?" he offered it to her.

After her experience moments before, she wasn't sure she ever wanted to touch a cigarette again in her life. "No, thank you."

"I'm not going to bullshit you," he told her after he had fired one up and took a long inhale from it.

"I'm glad." And she was. She was sick of bullshit in her life; she was working on clearing out the bullshit.

"Whoever this Clinton guy is wants you back in a bad way. He's willing to use Travis' cousin and my sister." He let that sink in for a few moments; let her really understand the gravity of the situation. It wasn't like he was picking on her because he had no one else to talk to. She held the key as to what this man wanted, and she refused to talk about it. "I want to know what you know—every single detail. You got that?"

"There's no need to talk to her like she's a fucking idiot." Travis took exception to the tone that Liam used.

Liam's eyes cut over to his communications officer, his face hard, his tone harder. "I can do this either with or without you, my man. I was polite in letting you sit in on this."

The thinly veiled threat did nothing to make Travis feel better. In fact, it increased his anxiety. She didn't deserve this shit, not after everything she'd already been through, but it wouldn't help to talk back or down to Liam either. He would throw him out faster than he could open his mouth and then talk to her however he wanted to. "I know." The thank you wasn't implied and it went unsaid.

She took a deep breath and looked inside herself for some fountain of energy she didn't know that she had. She had never planned to tell anyone anything about Clinton Herrington. Once she had escaped, she figured she would live her whole life looking over her shoulder, but she never figured she'd have to relive the things that he had done, what he had put her through. As she began to speak, her mind drifted back to the scene that she spoke about.

"I don't want to marry him!" she screamed at the top of her lungs. Her father, her own flesh and blood, had all but sold her to this man. There had even been a contract written up and signed between the two of them. Slave trading had been outlawed for hundreds of years, but it was apparently alive and well in Kentucky. She wondered what in the world her father had gotten her into.

He sighed, slapping the end of his belt in his hand. "Christine." The way he said her name spoke of boredom and impatience. "You know that it hasn't been cheap for us to raise you. God blessed us when Edward left the way he did."

"His name is Jagger." She tilted her chin up in defiance.

"His Godly name is Edward, and you will call him that."

There was silence between the two of them as a battle of wills ensued. Finally, she had to break eye contact, she couldn't stand it anymore. How could a parent do this to their own child? How could he wish one dead and then sell the other one off?

"What will I do?" she asked, her voice small and scared.

"You will service him, just like a wife is supposed to. You've read the Good Book, just as I have."

His version and her version were definitely not the same, but it had always been that way. Elias Stone had always seen things the way he wanted to see them; he'd always been a master manipulator, especially when it came to the Good Book.

"I just don't think that's what it says, Dad." She dared not look back into his eyes. He might smite her. He had done it before, numerous times. That was one of the reasons Jagger had left as soon as he turned eighteen.

"Are you talking back to me?" he yelled.

She felt moisture on her face. He had spit on her. "No, sir," she said softly. It was the only thing she could do.

"Then you will go upstairs, pack a bag, and then come meet your husband."

"What did you do?" Liam asked, as he let her have a breather.

"I did what he told me to do. I was so tired, tired of walking around on eggshells, tired of being knocked down, tired of being talked down to. I thought that maybe, for once, I had gotten a better end of the deal than he knew. I mean, I had snuck romance novels from the library." She sniffed as unexpected tears came to her eyes. "For once I decided to be optimistic. It was the absolute worst mistake of my life."

The man who had come to get her hadn't spoken one word to her since he'd picked her and her bag up from her family home. It was very disconcerting. She wasn't sure what to do with this. The man was much older than she had been lead to believe, and now she was nervous.

"Go inside and have a seat at the kitchen table," he told her. The first words he'd spoken to her. They were coarse and demanding, telling her that he wanted no argument from her. It was the same kind of tone her father used with her, and she absolutely hated it.

After she had a seat, a woman came over to her and pulled her up by the hand. The woman wasn't much older than she was. "I need your clothes," she told Christine. "And you need to take your hair down."

For the next two hours, she was poked and prodded. Her clothes were long gone, as was her modesty. She had been waxed—everywhere—and her hair had even been dyed. It was now a garish white color. And she was given contacts that made her eyes even bluer.

Looking at herself in the only mirror she was given, she realized that she looked like a young girl, almost like a doll. She'd been made into something that she wasn't. "Why did you do this?" she asked the woman who had brought her back to the room and performed all the rituals on her.

"Because it's what Clinton likes."

That first night, she was introduced to a lot of what Clinton liked, even more throughout the next few weeks. He married her seven days after she came to live with him. Two months after that was when the other girls started disappearing.

"What happened to them?" Liam asked her, running a hand over his face. This went a lot deeper than any of them knew. It went deeper than he'd wanted to get involved in.

"I don't know." She shrugged, her face blank. "I like to think that they got away, but I'm almost certain one of two things happened to all of them."

"What's that?" Travis asked as he reached over and grabbed her hand, trying to soothe her.

"There were other men who came around. I think what we were was a ring, not necessarily pornography, we were all of age."

"That's bullshit," Liam spit out. "Pornography is pornography, no matter how old you are. But what I think you were part of was more like slave trade."

She had thought that many times while she had been "learning her lesson" from Clinton, but she had been afraid to say it. If she said it, it meant it was true, and if there was one thing she had learned, it was if you said words, you gave them power. It could be good power or bad power, but either way, it gave them something over other people.

"You said one thing happened or another, what was

the other?" Travis asked, although he had a pretty good idea. People who did things like this didn't want there to be witnesses.

That same look came over her face again.

"Have you seen Tracy?" she asked one of the other girls as she folded the laundry for the house.

"Not in the past few days. She was supposed to go with Clinton to Cumberland Falls. He came back last night, but I haven't seen her."

Christine's blood ran cold. Tracy was her friend, and at night, the two of them had taken to whispering about what they would do when they were finally out of this house. They knew they couldn't be made to stay here forever. One day, someone would come and find them. They both held on strong to that belief. It was the only thing that helped them make it through. This time, Christine had a very bad feeling. As she opened her mouth to say something, Clinton came into the room and handed them a towel with blood on it.

"That's going to need to be disposed of. The cat got run over," he mentioned, as an afterthought.

When he left, they looked at the towel, neither one of them wanting to touch it. Neither one of them believed that the cat had gotten run over, especially when the aforementioned cat came in the room after Clinton had left. Finally, with tears streaming down her face, Christine took the towel and threw it in with the other whites, pouring bleach over the top of it. It was then that she knew she had to leave; she had to figure out a way to get out. She knew that if she didn't, she would die.

"Jesus Christ," Travis breathed.

"One by one, the girls disappeared, and another cat got run over, until I was the only one left," she whispered.

"So you can pin this on him," Liam finished for her. "You have just enough to pin a handful of murders on this man. Not to mention, I think we can all agree that he was doing some sort of slave trading."

"I have a ton of questions," Travis said. "How did he keep this quiet? How does no one else know about him?"

"Do I have to answer anymore right now?"

The two men had a good look at her. She was pale and her eyes were drawn tight. "No," Travis answered for the two of them. "You're good for now. Let me take you back to the clubhouse, and then Liam and I can meet with the rest of them and figure out what we're going to do."

"What about Jagger?" she asked.

At some point, and that point was going to be soon, they were going to have to deal with him. "We'll deal with it tomorrow," he told her. "Right now, I think all of us need to sleep on this. You've given us a lot to think about."

She'd also given herself a lot to think about. She wasn't sure exactly what she wanted anymore, but she was very happy that she wouldn't have to go through this by herself. Even a little bit of support was better than no support at all.

Chapter Thirteen

Travis sat in his cave later that night, checking on Heaven Hill's interests. As he scanned the cameras, he saw a car pull up to Roni's apartment building. It wasn't unusual for someone to park in her other parking spot, but this car looked familiar. Doing what he did best, he tapped into the Wi-Fi of the apartment building's security cameras and zoomed in.

"Well, I'll be damned," he chuckled.

Rooster was making his way up the sidewalk, and miracle of all miracles, he wasn't dressed in his sheriff's uniform. Dare he say that Rooster looked like he was about to go out on a date? He shook his head as Roni let his cousin in and quickly shut the door.

He clicked out of that feed and took a look at everything else. It all looked closed up for the night, and he was exhausted. The last few weeks had taken a lot out of him, and all he wanted to do was close his eyes for a week and catch up on all the sleep that he missed. It wasn't unusual for him to go on little sleep, but it was starting to take a toll. Shutting down everything but the essentials, he set the alarms and took one final sweep of his cave. He usually checked his feelings before he shut the door. Did he feel like he could go to his dorm room for a few hours? Was he at ease? Usually if he wasn't, something was going to happen. Tonight he was thankful that he was at ease.

When Travis made his way back to his dorm room, he felt odd. He'd had women in his dorm before, but never any that felt like this. He actually cared what she thought, wanted to make her happy in his own way. Should he knock on the door? Was it okay for him to just to walk in? Had Christy decided to move to an unoccupied room? They did have some of those. He hadn't shown them to her, but someone else could have. Glancing at the black watch he wore on his right wrist, he saw that it was later than he had meant for it to be. Opening the door slowly, he tried to be quiet as he walked into the room.

"Travis, is that you?" she asked, sitting up in the bed.

Her voice was soft, but it wasn't sleepy, the way he had assumed it would. Maybe she had been sitting up waiting on him? Maybe thinking the same things that he had been thinking. Fuck, she was in his bed. What the hell was he going to do now? "Yeah, it's me." he answered.

There was an awkward silence between the two of them. He wasn't prepared for this. Didn't mean at all that he didn't want it, but he wasn't sure he was prepared. There were a million things about her that he didn't know, some things he was downright scared to find out. It was all so up in the air.

When he didn't say anything, she cleared her throat and pulled the sheet up closer to her neck. It gave her a sense of security, as if he wouldn't be able to see the way she felt if she held that blanket up. Being here, amongst his things, had pulled some feelings to the surface that she hadn't known were possible. "I didn't know if you wanted me to be here..." She let the sentence fall off, embarrassment making her stop talking.

"No, you're fine. If you don't want me here, I can go stay in one of the other rooms that no one is in right now," he told her, putting his hands in the pockets of his jeans. He had never been this nervous around a woman, not even when he had been a young kid. He rocked back on his heels and waited for her to let him know how she wanted to play this. Hardly ever would he defer to someone else to tell him who could sleep in his room, but she had already been through so much. It was like Tyler had told him; he had to direct her in an easy way. He wanted her to stay, and if it was her decision, all the more better for it.

"I don't want to kick you out of your own room and bed. If you'll let me know which rooms are empty, I'll go take one." The moment the words came out of her mouth, she wanted to shove them back in. What had happened to the fearless woman from the night before? The one who had known exactly what Travis could see and had given him a free show? Why was she being a fraidy cat now?

He could see her from the light that she had left on in the bathroom. She was modestly covered in a pair of sleep pants and a T-shirt. Her hair was disheveled, and a thought crossed his mind that he wished he had been the one to do the disheveling. Even though her voice hadn't been laced with sleep, he could tell by the look in her eye that she was getting to the sleepy stage of the night. Probably made him a bastard, but he had watched her often enough on a computer screen to know what she looked like. He wanted desperately to know what she looked like lying beside him.

"You don't have to leave," he told her, his voice low, as not to scare her.

Christine hadn't expected him to say that. It wasn't that she didn't think he didn't desire her, she knew that he did, but this was his room. The one thing that was his in this whole world besides the motorcycle he rode on and the patch on his back. "You want me to stay?"

That was the bitch of it, wasn't it? He did want her to stay, but he didn't want to force her to make a decision that she wasn't ready for. "I want you to do whatever you want to do. I'm not that guy that tells you what you have to do. I've never been that kind of guy. I will tell you this, though. I'm gonna go take a shower. When I come out, you can either be here or not. There will be no hard feelings on my part if you aren't here."

That seemed fair enough to the both of them. It took the pressure off just enough that she could breathe.

He could feel her eyes on him as he went about the room, gathering the stuff he would need. From where he stood, he could almost hear the thoughts rushing through her head, and he worried if he hurried this, what if she wasn't ready and what if he did irreparable damage to their tenuous, at best, relationship? "No hard feelings," he told her again as he went into the bathroom and shut the door.

The click that indicated the door was shut sounded like a cannon going off in the silence of the room. She paced a circle around the bed and a couch that sat in the corner as she thought about what he had offered her. It was the best of both worlds, and there was no pressure behind any of it, she knew that without a doubt, but the implications were still there. The feelings were there, even if they were there only on her part. That's what she had always been led to believe—men desired, but they didn't feel anything else for women. They wanted property, and she wasn't stupid, she knew what motorcycle clubs were; she had seen a property patch on a woman before. There was a part of her that wasn't sure if she would be happy wearing that, not after what all she had already been through.

Then there was the elephant in the room. Jagger. He was going to flip his shit when he found out how long this had been going on and he'd had no clue. She was sure of that, but a part of her wanted him to get angry. A part of her wanted him to know exactly how rough it had been for her with him gone. That was the selfish part of her personality, the part that she hadn't let surface in a very long time. "It's not his fault," she whispered to herself. And it wasn't, but knowing that did nothing to help her sleep at night.

There had been so many nights she had prayed that he would come find her, be the big brother that she remembered him being. She had dreams that he would come to the front door and knock it down, trying to get to her. When she had been little, he had promised her that nothing would ever happen to her, that he would protect her at all costs. In this he had failed miserably, and she did wonder if he had ever thought of her again. Had he wondered where she was? Had he thought about what their father had done to her?

Pushing all those feelings aside was hard, but Christine

knew that what Travis asked of her had nothing to do with Jagger. It had to do with what she wanted the two of them to be. Did she want them to sleep in the same bed? Did she want to be able to count on him to help her and her help him in return? That was something that had been sorely lacking in their relationship previous to this. Travis had done all the helping, and she had allowed it to happen, never offering, never anticipating what he might need from her. But that was where she got confused. The men in her life before him would need sex…did Travis need sex? Did he want it with her? He desired her, yes, but she didn't know what he felt inside. Biting her thumbnail, she exhaled deeply and realized that she had run out of time. She could no longer hear the shower running inside the bathroom, and the doorknob was turning.

She stood rooted to the spot as Travis came out, steam and hot air billowing around him. "You're still here?"

"Don't act so surprised," she tried the joke out. It was a little funny—it was something that she could definitely work on and with.

"No, I am, I figured you would be long gone, in another room by now."

Her eyes landed on his bare chest, and she fought not to stare. Clinton had been an older man, and while Travis' stomach and chest weren't as muscular as some of the others she had seen working at *Wet Wanda's*, he was very good looking to her. On one pectoral, he had a large tattoo. She had seen the ones on his arms before, but this one was different. This was one that he purposely kept hidden from other people, and it could only be seen because he had chosen to take his shirt off in your presence. She took that sentiment and held it close to her heart. It felt good, it felt right.

"You okay?" he asked, his voice held a twinge of laughter as she pulled her eyes away from him.

"I've just never seen you without a shirt on before." That sounded lame even to her own ears.

"I don't parade around like some people do without one on. I don't have a lot to show off."

But to her he did, and she wanted so badly to call it her own. What would he say if she told him that?

Chapter Fourteen

L ying down in the bed together had been one of the most awkward things that either one of them had ever experienced. The tension was so thick that it could have been cut with a knife.

"Is lying in bed with a man always this awkward?" she asked softly as she turned to face Travis, careful not to touch him.

That comment struck him as odd, but he tried to make a joke anyway. "I don't know, I've never been in bed with a man before. Besides, you were married."

She still was married, but she hated to focus on that. "Yeah, but we never slept in the same bed together."

His eyebrow rose. "Never?" That was supposed to be one of the major perks of putting a ring on it. The fact that you could go to bed and reach over whenever you wanted to either be close or, if you were feeling the need, fuck her until you fell back asleep.

"Nope." She shook her head.

The sound of her hair moving against the sheet was loud in the stillness of the room.

"He only came to visit me for, what do prisoners call it? Conjugal visits? Then he would leave as soon as he was done."

There seemed to be no finesse. He wondered if she had even liked it. Had she ever found pleasure in anything besides the touch of her own hand? He hadn't realized he'd asked her that question out loud until she answered.

"No, and do you know how much of a disadvantage that puts you at being a stripper?"

The laugh exploded from his body. Sometimes he could almost forget that she had been a stripper. "No."

She huffed and resituated herself. "The whole time I was there, Wanda would tell me, 'You must look sexier. Imagine the way you look at your husband. How do you feel when he gives you an orgasm? Give the men that face.'"

He waited patiently for her to continue. He was afraid he would embarrass her if he asked any more questions.

"But I had never had one. When I finally told Jasmine, Jasmine took me to a store just north of here, and we made a ton of purchases. I had to figure it out on my own," she whispered.

Those words went straight to his gut, and then that tension was back. Travis cleared his throat. "I don't know what to say to that."

She laughed. "You don't have to say anything, I'm just being honest."

He needed to be honest too. He wanted to be the first guy to do that for her. Being turned down, though, would make things very uncomfortable between the two of them. In the end, he just decided to go for it. If she didn't want it, she didn't want it, but if she did, then maybe it would be the tipping point that would make her finally be able to fully trust and believe in him.

One minute, she was lying back against the pillow and Travis was lying beside her. The next minute, Travis had scooted over next to her, his face next to hers. "If I do anything that you don't like, you tell me."

She nodded.

"I need to hear you say it." He didn't want to scare her, he didn't want anything at all to be misconstrued, he had to know that she wanted this as much as he did.

"Okay, I trust you."

Those words were everything that he had always wanted to hear from her. He couldn't believe how good it felt, how it made his heart race to hear that. They made him feel like motherfucking Superman, but there was still that inner debate—should he get on top of her, should he just stay on his side, facing her? He wished he was as smooth as some of the other members of the club. Fucking hell, Travis, just do whatever Tyler would do, he told himself. Never in his life had he been this nervous with a woman.

Christine must have seen the hesitation in his eyes, the personal battle he was having with himself, because she grabbed his cheeks and pulled his face closer to hers before placing a soft kiss on his lips. It was quick and she pulled back just as quickly.

"I trust you."

He moved a lot quicker than he meant to, stretching himself over her body, holding himself up with his hands flat on the mattress. "I don't deserve that trust."

Christine looped her arms around his neck, burying her fingers in the hair there. "You do. You're the only one I've trusted in such a long time. I want you to understand that. You're the only person that I've been able to be myself with—ever. I'm still trying to figure out who that is, but I feel at peace when I'm with you, I've never felt at peace before."

There were no words for what she had just told him, he didn't know how to process it, how to tell her that he was himself around her too. More than he'd ever been. In the club, he got lost because he was quiet, because his presence wasn't demanding. He wasn't physically intimidating like the rest of them. It was his mind that made him dangerous, the things he could do with words and computer code. His threat was much quieter, but just as effective—not everyone understood that. The ones that did, knew exactly what he did for the club; the ones that didn't sold him short and saw him as weak. Here, with her in his arms, he felt like the strongest man in the world.

Not being able to take the feelings that were rushing through his body, he dipped his head down, brushing her lips with his. Her reaction was tentative, and he didn't want to rush it, but he had to taste her. With equally slow movements, he pried her mouth open with the tip of his tongue. She gasped into the kiss, and he wasn't sure that she liked it until she arched her back, pressing her breasts into his chest. Her nails at the back of his neck dug into the skin there. The bite of pain was welcome as he braced himself up on one arm and used the other to cup her face and tilt her chin so he could use her mouth just the way he wanted to. In this movie between the two of them, he was the director, and he showed her with gentle pressure what he wanted.

"Travis," she whispered when he broke the kiss. He tilted her chin up, trailing his lips along her jawline, down to her neck.

Christine had never done anything like this before. There had been no finesse when she was with Clinton. There had never been slow kisses, a buildup to anything. It was always he told her to be waiting in bed with her clothes off, and he would come to her, do his business, and be done. He'd kissed her maybe four times in the entire length of time she'd been there. This was entirely new territory for her. His lips and teeth nipped at her neck, his tongue soothing the burn when he put a small amount of pressure behind it.

"You okay?" he asked as his kisses trailed up to her ear.

She shivered when he used his teeth to nip her earlobe, a ribbon of excitement running through her body, causing her to arch against him. "Yeah." She was afraid to move her hands from around his neck, afraid that she would make the wrong move and this would all be over. It felt too good. His mouth was now back at her neck, but this time it was at the column of her throat, and he was moving down, closer to her chest. Involuntarily, she felt her nipples harden against the cotton of her T-shirt, and she wanted him to lift it off her body, to show herself to him. She'd only showed herself to the men at *Wet Wanda's*. This was something that she had a choice in, and she wanted desperately to show him that she chose him.

Lifting the lids of her eyes so that they were open, she looked down. His dark head was moving even further down her body, and the hand that had been at her jaw was now at the hem of her T-shirt. She'd never realized how big his hands were until one was splayed against her stomach, pushing the fabric up. It came to a stop just below her breast, and he took that moment to look up at her. His eyes were dark, full of desire. She'd never seen anything like it before, and she knew without a doubt that she wanted to see this look from him again; she had to see it again. She would do anything to see this look from him as many times as she could throughout her life. The look was so vulnerable, so full of emotion. In that moment she lost her heart to him. It had been hovering in his hands for a long time—the way he took care of her and the way she trusted him…it had been coming. But it was that bare, vulnerable gaze he gave her that clenched it all.

"Can I take this off?"

The tone of voice he used was quiet and respectful, telling her that if she wasn't comfortable, it would be okay to tell him so, and he would be fine with that. The level of understanding he had with her was one she had never in her life been given with anyone else. Tears clogged her throat for some unknown reason, but she knew that she didn't want to ruin this.

"Please."

The side of his mouth tilted in a cocky grin.

She helped him when he struggled using his one hand, and they both laughed. When his brown eyes swept her body, she fought not to cover herself up with one of her arms. It was difficult, but she didn't. Insecurities came up from places that she hadn't counted on.

"What's wrong? You tensed."

He was so in-tune with everything involving her that she had to take another moment to thank the God that sent him to her—and she hadn't thanked God for anything in a while. "What if I'm no good at this?"

A mischievous smile lit up his face. "Then we practice until you feel like you get it right."

She laughed, the sound loud in the room, but it filled him up with pride. He had successfully put her at ease. Not waiting for her to question anything else, he moved his hand from her stomach to the side of her breast. He watched her eyes as he stroked his thumb over the nub there. She inhaled deeply. "We good?" he asked.

"Yeah." She breathed harder as he stroked a few more times, each pass faster than the last.

He nodded, dipping his head down, and instead of his thumb, this time, his tongue snaked out. Christine shifted so hard she almost came up off the bed, and he worried that maybe he had done something wrong.

"I'm fine," she panted. But she really wasn't. She wanted more and wasn't sure how to tell him. Everything that Travis was doing was causing a deep ache in the middle of her body, the same kind of ache that she got late at night when she thought of him. She wanted him to take care of it, she was sick of taking care of it herself. She gripped his hair in her fingers and thrust against him. "More," she whispered.

"What?" he asked, not sure that he had heard her correctly.

"I need more," she breathed out, the frustration causing her to disentangle her hands from his hair and tangle them in her own, holding it back from her face. She was hot, so hot, and she needed him to make her even hotter. That was the only way she would cool off. "Don't treat me like I'm gonna break."

There was an internal war with himself, how much did she mean of the words that she said and how much of it was desire talking? He hesitated.

"I'm serious. I want this to be with you, I want to feel it with you." She steeled herself against the words she was about to say, they were so unlike her. "Give me the first orgasm I haven't had at my own fingers."

Chapter Fifteen

Their deep breathing was the only sound in the room as the gravity of what she said struck him in the chest. He was startled for a moment, and then he realized what she had actually said to him. "Yes, ma'am."

Christine sucked in a deep breath as he attacked her with an aggression that she hadn't thought him capable of. Instead of the easy petting, the light tongue against her skin, this time he went after her hard. The stubble on his cheeks rubbed harshly against her skin, and she knew that she would wear that burn like a badge of honor, even if nobody but her could see it. His teeth worried the soft skin around her nipple. She gasped as his tongue soothed it, the slippery warmth of his mouth was a feeling she'd never felt before, and she strained against him.

From where he worked, he tilted his eyes up, watching the look on her face. He noticed that she gripped her hair tightly, almost like she was afraid to touch him. He wondered if she thought she would break the spell if she did. Travis was trying to man up; he knew that once he went this far with her, he wouldn't ever be able to come back from the precipice. He would go over and he would be done for. When he loved, he loved hard, and he knew that this woman—she could kill him and he'd go easily.

He let go of her skin and slid up her body so that they were on eye level. "You're gonna kill me, you know this, right?" he asked, a soft grin on his face.

"No, I don't." She shook her head, not sure what he meant.

Travis never broke her gaze as he let his hand trail down her stomach and over the only barrier that kept him from touching the part of her he wanted the most.

Her eyes dilated as she got what he meant, and she spread her legs to accommodate him. She felt the tips of his fingers brush against the side of her underwear, and then bare skin, and she sucked in a breath. Without warning, his finger brushed against her clit, and she bucked against him, her eyes closing.

"Nope, Christy, stay with me," he told her. "Open those eyes."

This was a lot for her, way more intimate than anything she'd ever participated in before. It was hard for her to open up her emotions like this, but she knew that she needed to. She knew that it wasn't fair to him to keep herself closed off because that's what she always did. Opening her eyes was one of the hardest things she had ever done.

"There ya go," he praised her, gritting his teeth against the feelings coursing through his own body. Her core was hot and wet and it was inviting, and he wanted so badly to shove himself there and put both of them out of their misery, but he kept going back to WWTD? Tyler would make sure that his woman was taken care of and worry about himself later.

"Travis," she whined as he worked against her, not letting up. The feelings were overwhelming as she tried to process them. She had never allowed anyone else to make her feel this way before, never given herself over to anyone else. It was scary, sexy, and amazing, all at the same time.

He watched her face, not able to look away as he manipulated her pleasure for himself. This wasn't the kind of relationship where he took just what he wanted. He had been in those, more often than he cared to admit to anyone, but he wanted this more for her. The willingness to make sure she was pleasured in spite of his own needs was something new for him. It was those feelings that kept him here, in this limbo with her. But that wasn't something to think about now; all he wanted to think about now was getting her there, pushing her over that edge, so that he could be the one who owned her pleasure. Nobody had ever given her this before, and he was going to be the one to own this part of her.

She sucked her bottom lip between her teeth and bit down hard. "Feel good?" he asked, although he knew the answer. Her body was now pliant. When he'd first entered her, it had been tighter.

"Yes!" She strained against him and her brows furrowed. She was reaching, reaching for the spot that was just out of her grasp.

"What do you need?" he asked, his voice hot against her ear.

"Can you talk to me?" Her face burned with embarrassment even asking the question, but she found with him she wanted the experience to be good. She no longer wanted to wonder why everyone else loved this so much.

He stopped for a nanosecond, presumably to catch his breath and process her request. "Do you know how fucking hot you are to me? I've wanted to do this since the first moment I saw you on the stage at *Wet Wanda's*. There hasn't been one day that I have been around you that I haven't wondered what this would be like."

"Did I live up to it?" she asked as she ground her body against his hand.

He smirked, biting the edge of her earlobe. "Fucking crushed it."

It was that little bite of pain that pushed her over. She gasped loudly and went to put her hand over her mouth, the way she had before, but he grabbed it, forcing her to put sounds and words to her pleasure. Neither one of them was sure what she said, what she did, but it was enough to know that they shared the experience.

He turned them so that they faced one another, and they were quiet for a long time until she opened her mouth.

"I have to ask, this has been bothering me for a while, I'm not sure why, but I gotta know."

He gave her an indulgent smile. "What?"

"This hipster glasses that you sometimes wear…" He laughed before she could even finish. "Do you have to wear them or are they a fashion statement?"

"I'm one of those lucky fuckers that has 20/20 vision. I just wear them to piss Tyler off. He calls me a hipster too."

She wished she knew all these people in his life and, in turn, in Jagger's life. That was the one she missed, the closeness that she had once had with her brother. She wanted that back, but it would mean being honest with him and telling him the hell that she had been through. She hadn't even been able to tell Travis everything that had gone on.

"You okay?"

Christy nodded. "I just know that I'm going to have to see Jagger, face him, and tell him everything, and I know it's going to have to be soon. Probably tomorrow."

He knew that too. With Rooster breathing down their backs, there was no way they could keep this quiet much longer. It wasn't fair to continue to keep this to themselves, not when she was going to be staying at the dorm, and especially not when they were going to be right under Jagger's nose for the most part. It wasn't fair to any of them involved. "You're right. We should tell them tomorrow. The quicker we do it, the quicker we can figure out what these sheriffs want with you, and we can defuse the situation with Roni, Rooster, and Liam."

"This is going to cause major problems, isn't it?"

Travis wanted to lie and tell her that it wouldn't, that they were all adults and they should be able to behave that way, but he couldn't. Jagger could be a hot head, and truth be told, so could he. He wasn't sure how this was going to play out, but he couldn't lie to her. "I don't know. I hope not, but I can't promise anything. None of us are known for our level-headedness. Except for maybe Tyler. He can be level-headed unless it deals with Mer. If it deals with her, then all bets are off."

"I don't want to make this difficult for you." She reached up and put her hand on his cheek, running it along the stubble that grew there. "That was never my intention."

"Believe it or not, I know that. I'm the one who chased

after you. If it hadn't been for your car breaking down on the side of the road that day, then I would never have found you."

She remembered that day and then the subsequent days after that, when she had been scared of her own shadow but still stripping because she had needed money. She'd worried every time she saw him at *Wet Wanda's* that he had told Jagger. Then weeks later, he'd come to her with another job, one where she wouldn't have to take her clothes off, and she'd questioned everything about him again. No one had ever been that nice to her. Every time someone gave her something, it was because they wanted something in return. Even when he had put her up in the house to get her out of the CRISIS center, she still hadn't believed he was doing it because he cared for her. Somewhere in the back of her mind, she always wondered when the shoe was going to drop, when he was going to tell her that he was done playing games and they were adults, and that he wanted payment for his services. Those days and words, though, they never came. He never once asked for anything.

"I'm glad you did find me, but I feel like I've been taking advantage of you." She took a deep breath. "Which is why I want to be the one to tell Jagger."

He knew immediately that wasn't a good idea—at all. "No, we need to do it together."

She knew her brother, but it occurred to her that she knew the brother that he had been then and not the man that he was now. It had been a very long time. "I think I'll be fine, and I feel like I owe it to all of us to be the one to do this. I keep putting you out, and I don't want to be that girl."

"You aren't that girl," he argued. "Anything I've done, I've done because I wanted to."

"But at the same time, I've let you. Now it's time for me to stand on my own two feet."

"If this is what you want to do, then that's fine, but I want to be there. I need to be there. If he gets out of hand, then I will handle him. I'm not throwing you to the wolves on your first day." He shook his head at her. "I wouldn't do that to my worst enemy, and I like you way more than I've ever liked anyone else."

Those words warmed a spot in her heart that had long been cold, and she held them close. "Then it's agreed? You let me tell him, but you can be there."

"I'll let you tell him, but I promise you, when he starts swingin'—which he will do—it will be at me."

Christine didn't want any more violence, and she hoped against it all that Travis was wrong about that.

Chapter Sixteen

Every grand plan the two of them had about how to tell Jagger was destroyed the very next morning. He wasn't supposed to be anywhere near the clubhouse, Travis had been absolutely sure of that. He was supposed to be at the shop, fixing Cash's car. Travis had verified that with more than one person. So to say he was surprised when Jagger walked in, his arm around B, as Travis was telling Christine where they kept breakfast stuff was an understatement.

The silence in the room was deafening. Travis had never understood the meaning of that phrase before, but as Jagger's eyes went back and forth between him and Christine, the silence thundered in his ears. He could see the minute that Jagger put two and two together—it clicked in his eyes. The girls always talking about Travis having a woman, her being there this morning. He didn't say one word as Jagger growled and came at him. He side-stepped him, and grabbed Jagger by the wrist.

"How long have you known?" Jagger didn't even recognize his own voice coming out of his mouth. The words were garbled, the pain was fresh. He swung with his other arm.

"C'mon man," Travis told him, pulling him by the arm out the back door. "Let's not do this here, let's take it outside."

Jagger, however, was a solid guy and he was not budging. He stood his ground, yanking against the hold that Travis had on him. He got loose, and Tyler grabbed him by the shirt. "I asked you how long you've known," he yelled, pointing his finger at Travis.

He didn't want to do this in front of the rest of the group, the ladies, the children that had gathered around. This was private, this was between them, and he didn't want the rest of them to see it—especially Christine. Especially after what they had shared the night before. This was too much for all of them. He had known this was the way it would go down, there was no other way it could. Jagger had no time to ease into this, he had no time to gauge his pain, it spewed forth now.

"A while, and I'm not discussing it any further with you until we take it outside."

Jagger's face twisted. He fought against Tyler's hold. Tyler struggled to hang onto him, planting his feet on the floor and pulling back against gravity. "No, asshole, you don't get to tell me what to do. I can't believe you would hide this from me. That's my sister!"

Bianca reached for him as he broke free of Tyler's hands, but they all missed him, and it was then that Travis knew he was in trouble. He wouldn't defend himself because he knew he deserved it. Jagger hit him around the middle like a ton of bricks, knocking him into the table that stood in the middle of the room. They went down hard, and Travis struggled to catch his breath as they crashed into the floor, his head hitting the table, and he screamed bloody murder.

"Jagger!" He could hear the women yelling at him, both Bianca and Christine, telling him to stop, but he couldn't. He wanted Travis to know exactly how he felt. He had searched for his sister for years, had even gone back to their home and faced down his piece-of-shit father to find out what had happened to her. To find out she had been under his nose for months and he'd had no idea? That sucked, that hurt, and that was liable to make him rip Travis' head clear off his shoulders.

Travis could feel the blows as they came, one by one, with each crack of Jagger's knuckles, some of his guilt went away. All along he had known it was wrong, he knew that it would backfire and probably fizzle out, but he'd wanted this so badly. He refused to defend himself—he deserved every bit of this.

"Stop!" Bianca and Christine both yelled at Jagger.

Travis had snapped out of it and was now trying to defend himself because his head hurt and his vision was blurry. "Dude," he was telling Jagger. "Calm down, let's go talk about this."

"Talk? You fucking want me to talk to you? That's my sister!" The words seemed to enrage him even further.

Christine watched as Jagger beat the ever-loving shit out of Travis. She had given up trying to make him stop. Every time he heard her voice, he seemed to hit harder, and she didn't want that for Travis. This was all because of her, but she didn't know how to put an end to it.

Looking over at the man they called Rooster, she touched his arm. "Please, make him stop."

It was the way she looked at him, the way she made the appeal, that forced him to take a step forward and wrap his arms around Jagger's waist, pulling the two of them apart. "I think he's had enough."

Rooster was worried that Jagger wasn't done, so he stood behind him for a few more minutes, waiting for the other man to get his breath.

"He's had enough," Liam told Jagger. He had come running at the sound of screams, and he hadn't been sure what he would see once he got there. It surprised him. He had figured they would have told Jagger by now. "He's bleeding, you got his head good."

They helped Travis to sit up, but he slumped to the side when the room spun. "Fuck, man, he did get you good," Layne said as he lifted the hair on the back of Travis' head to get a good look at where the blood was coming from.

Christine ran up to her brother, pulling him around by the arm. "You could have killed him!"

They two of them came face to face for the first time in years, and the entire room was quiet. The tension was thick as the two of them looked at each other. Finally Jagger spoke, his voice harder than she had ever heard. He seemed like an entirely different person when the words left his mouth. "He's fuckin' lucky I didn't. I hoped you had gotten out, but in reality, I thought you were dead. Now I found out he's known where you've been, and he still won't tell me? For how long?" That was the one thing he needed to know. How long had this been going on?

"You left!" The minute the words were out of her mouth, she clamped her hand over her mouth, like she shouldn't have spoken the truth.

"No." Jagger shook his head, his eyes flashing. "Do not cover your mouth from speaking the truth. I might be a bastard, but I am nothing like him."

Only they knew who Jagger spoke of—their father. If they said anything that showed him in an unsavory light, even if it was the truth, they both knew they would be paying for it for days. Both of them had learned to keep their mouths shut, to bury their true feelings down deep, so that no one would know what they really were.

"Then can I speak freely?" she asked, her voice soft against the harshness of Travis' breath. Tyler and Layne were attending to him as she and Jagger were having their face-off.

"Please do." He never wanted her to be scared of him the way she had their father—the same way he had been, and the feeling that he had just done more damage than good weighed heavily on him.

"Let's go out here." She pointed to the sliding glass door that led to the back porch.

"Don't go out there with him by yourself," Travis told her from where he sat, but his words were slurred, and she worried that Jagger had hurt him badly.

She glanced behind her at Jagger and held up one finger before walking over to Travis. "I need to do this," she whispered when she had crouched down to his level.

"I don't feel comfortable with it," he argued, sounding more like himself.

She shook her head before she placed her hand on his shoulder. "All you've done since I met you is protect me and take care of me. This is something I want to do on my own, something I have to do on my own. This is between us and no one else."

He had to respect that. She was right; he had done as much as he could for her, now it was time for her to stand on her own. He would be just like her dad, just like Clinton, if he didn't let her do that. It was a small step, but a huge leap in what he was beginning to see was a recovery of sorts. "Alright."

His reward for agreeing to let her be her own person was a soft kiss on the cheek. She stood up and let Jagger escort her out the back door. Once they got there, neither one knew what to say. The silence between them had never been so strained, had never been so awkward, even when they were kids. They'd always had a million and one things to talk about. Those things weren't there anymore, and that made her heart hurt. For the first time, Christine realized she was going to have possibly live with the fact that she would no longer have a relationship with her brother.

Chapter Seventeen

Jagger finally broke the silence. His voice was low, the tone tortured. "Tell me. Just tell me everything that you went through. I need to hear it, and I don't want you to hold anything back. We need to get it out in the open if we're going to move past it."

Christine couldn't look at him when she spoke, so she turned, facing the backyard, focusing on the fence that surrounded the property. "The day you left, I knew that my life was over. I could tell in the way Dad looked at me, the things he said to me. He would get onto me if I ate what he deemed too much, if I didn't exercise the way he thought I should. I had a feeling he was grooming me for something, but I didn't know what. I waited, and waited, and the closer I got to eighteen the more nervous I got."

Jagger let out a deep breath and his stomach clenched. He wasn't going to like what she had to say, and he knew it, but he'd told her not to sugarcoat anything. If she had lived through it, he sure as hell could listen to it. He took a seat at the table and put his head in his hands.

"A week before my birthday, he told me to get ready. The day of my birthday, he told me to go upstairs and pack my stuff, that I was about to fulfill my duty as a woman."

"Were you scared?" He had to know, how had she felt?

It seemed like forever until she spoke again. "For a long time, I dreamed that you would come find me, because you knew how Dad was, you knew what kind of hell we were living in. At eighteen you could take me and I could say that I was fine with that. But it changed, the longer I was there, the more sure I was that you were never going to find me. I had to take the fear I did feel and turn it into something else. I used that feeling to get me out of the situation."

That tore Jagger's heart apart. He had gone back to their childhood home to try and find her. He'd been run off by the police, and he'd not been allowed back. A few months ago, he'd gone back at night and the place was abandoned. "I did look for you. I went back, and me and the old man had it out. I was escorted off by police and told never to come back. I had nothing to go on, and looking back, I probably should have asked Steele to find you for me. I had this idea, though, that maybe you had a better life, that maybe you were happy. I was afraid I would ruin it, and I didn't want to be the cause of that, especially after how we were raised up."

"It wasn't." She turned around to face him, the tears swimming in her eyes. "My life absolutely sucked. I am still married to a man that's almost 50 years old. I want to be divorced, but that means that I would have to tell him where I am. He's going to make my life a living hell for the rest of my life. He's already started, trying to use you against me with this information with the club. He wants me to come out of hiding."

"You're not going to," Jagger told her, his tone hard.

"I have to. He's not going to stop. Don't you understand that?" Her hands shook. "He's not going to stop until he gets me back. He's obsessed with me."

"Tell me, please. We can't protect you until you tell us."

"I've told Travis some."

That pissed him off. If she was confiding in anyone, it should be him. He knew that it was stupid for him to feel that way, he hadn't been a part of her life in years, but it still hurt. He had always been the one to protect her, and he wanted to be that person now. "But you haven't told me."

She shook her head, her face breaking. "It's embarrassing and shameful. I don't want you to think less of me." Tears streamed down her face. "Travis saw me at my absolute worst and helped me out. He didn't know me before, he's only known the broken me."

"That's not fair," he told her. "You haven't given me a chance to know the 'broken' you. But I can guarantee you; I've felt much of what you have. It's been a long journey for me to be with B. It took a lot of understanding and even therapy. If there's any place you could have come to be healed from being broken—it's here. Nobody in that room has had an easy life. Nobody. Not many people know what's happened to Steele, but we just found out that he and Rooster are cousins, so it's pretty obvious that he also has his own demons. We help each other here."

She was quiet for so long that he thought he'd lost her, that she wasn't going to open up to him. Just when he was about to give up, she started to speak. "I was his slave. Not in the housework sense of the word. I did that too, but I did it to keep from being bored. His brand of enslavement was sexual. He asked sexual favors of me and expected me to perform whenever he wanted me to."

"Did he hurt you?"

Christine knew that she had to be honest. "Sometimes. There were a few times that I fought him and he beat me up or hurt me badly."

"When did it start?"

"Our wedding night," she smiled sadly. "There were other women too, but they disappeared the longer I was there."

"Do you know what happened to them?"

"Not really." She shrugged. "I know that I was his favorite, and I'm kind of afraid that he killed them," she let that fact slip through quietly. It felt freeing to tell someone else.

Jagger's mind was working a mile a minute. "How the hell did he get away with it?"

"Clinton had friends, law enforcement friends. At least two or three times a month, there was a sheriff car parked out in front of the house. I never saw the actual people, but the cars belonged to different counties. I get the feeling he had something on all of them. One night he had a huge fight with one of them, and I could hear some of the words as they screamed at each other. It's like he finds the one weakness that the person has and he exploits it. Just like he did with you guys. It's something that you can't get out of easily or something that you can't just push under the rug." She was quiet for a few minutes. "I think that's how he got me. He knew something about Dad. He mentioned once when he was drunk, which was rare, about something that happened with someone involving the church and how it was swept under the rug."

Jagger froze and his body turned cold. "That wasn't Dad," he whispered. "That was me."

That pissed him off. This piece of shit had used what had happened to him against his sister? How had this man even found out about it? How long had he been looking at Christine before he'd approached their dad to marry her? Was he a child molester? So that she would understand that he wasn't the one who'd had to hide, he forged ahead. "Something was done to me. I didn't do anything that had to be covered up, it was done to me, and Dad didn't want to believe it. There were certain people that did, though. Of course, Dad wanted to sweep it under the rug and not let people know what happened."

"Then we were both played," she whispered.

"Because we had awesome parents." His tone was sarcastic.

"But it didn't kill us," she grinned as she walked over and put her hand in his.

"Nope, it didn't. Here the two of us are, still standing. I actually have a woman that loves me, I know you've got a man that cares deeply for you, and I'm really sorry that I busted his head open. It was such a shock to see you. I didn't know what to do. All I thought was how long I've looked for you and he'd had you all along. It pissed me off."

"Can you imagine how I felt when I started stripping at *Wet Wanda's* and I found out that my brother was the one bringing the house down singing? I wondered why in the world, out of anywhere that I could have gone, I went to the place you were."

"Because it always works out, no matter what."

For the first time in a long time, she actually believed him.

Travis' head was killing him, and he wasn't looking forward to Jagger coming back into the clubhouse. It had gone even worse than he had assumed it would.

"Are you okay?" Rooster asked as he sat next to his cousin.

"Do I look okay?" he asked, pulling away the towel from the back of his head. They were waiting on Ashley to get there to stitch him up.

Rooster was quiet for a few minutes before he spoke. "I'm sorry you got caught up in my shit."

"What?" His head hurt, and he wasn't able to figure out what in the hell Rooster was going on about. "It may be the fact that my head is pounding, but you're going to have to explain to me what you mean by that."

"If I hadn't done what I did as a teenager, with Roni and Liam, this Clinton man wouldn't have been able to use it against Christine. I'm sorry about that."

"This is what I don't get, Brandon." It felt weird, using Rooster's given name. It had been a very long time since he'd used it, since they were kids. "Why weren't you honest with me about why you and Liam didn't talk anymore? Why aren't you true to yourself? Obviously you're just as outlaw as the rest of the guys in this clubhouse."

"It's hard to explain, but I had to take on a persona to keep myself safe at that camp. Liam thinks that maybe he had it worse in juvie, but I wonder about that every day of my life. The people up there at that camp were hardcore. It was the last place they were going before prison, and they were hard ass about all of it. Every day that I was there, I wished that someone would come get me and take me home. I was made fun of because of my red hair, because I had made a deal and Liam had been sent to juvie and I hadn't. Everyone knew what had happened."

Travis remembered, it had been a big deal back then. It had been on the news, and there had been talk that they would be tried as adults. Everyone had a theory about what had really happened. There was talk that William had actually done it and then let his son and Rooster take the fall for it. Lots of people in their small town thought it was Liam's initiation, that it was the only way he would be allowed into the Heaven Hill MC. Knowing now what that event had really been, Travis was sad. It had ruined a friendship, and now it was affecting lives of people that hadn't even known about it.

"So you decided to become a hard ass and be a sheriff's deputy?"

"I didn't know what else to do. After I completed the program, my record was expunged, and I was scared. Believe it or not, a lot of people wanted to be the ones to break me. I needed something to do that would show me how to protect myself in a legal way. Then once I got there, I had to change the way I thought. I was used to hanging out with people who didn't necessarily obey the law, and then here I was expected to uphold it. It wasn't nearly as easy for me as people assumed, I'll tell you that. There's a large, very large, part of me that would love to be in the position you are. That's honestly where my heart is."

"With Roni?" Travis grinned.

"That was a long time ago, but you never forget the first, huh?" Rooster couldn't keep the sad smile off his face either. "There are going to be some tough decisions I'm going to have to make, but first I need to figure out what we're going to do about this Clinton guy. He wants your lady back, in a bad way, and he's got something on the sheriff. I'm not sure I can help with this. My hands might be tied."

"Then we have to figure out what he has on the sheriff or figure out something on him. But first, you need to talk to Christine, she thinks there were some women killed in that house, and I need to get a motherfucking painkiller." He winced.

Rooster pulled his cuffs out of their holder. "You want me to arrest Jagger for assault?" He couldn't keep the smile off his face.

Travis laughed. "If only that would bring this asshole out into the open."

"It might," Rooster mumbled, thinking aloud. "If he wants Christine, don't you think he would know who her brother is? Wouldn't he be interested in a having a few minutes alone with him?"

"No," a female voice yelled. "Don't use him like that."

Christine and Jagger had come back in, and they had obviously caught the tail end of the conversation.

Jagger spoke up. "Do you think it would help? Cause you can go ahead and put me in those cuffs if you think it will."

Rooster turned it over in his head for a couple of

minutes. "I think it's worth a shot. What's one night there? We'll keep you by yourself, and come tomorrow morning we'll drop the charges and you'll be free to go. What have we got to lose?"

"He's not a nice man. I know exactly what he can do if he gets you alone."

"You forget what I've been doing the past few years, sis," Jagger reminded her. "I can handle myself. It's not that big of a deal."

She took a glance around the clubhouse and, for the first time, really looked at the people who were surrounding them. She guessed he had been doing a lot of different things in the last few years. There was not one person here who looked like they couldn't handle themselves. It was time for her to ask for help, time for her to let her brother in and put this part of life behind her. It was time for her to live, and it was her right. She didn't have to stay the way she had been. It was okay to make a change.

"Okay, but whatever he tells you about me, don't believe him."

She was very well aware of how he liked to manipulate, and she was scared that he would turn them all against her, right as she had found them.

Chapter Eighteen

Christine sighed as she sat on the same back porch that she had been on earlier in the day. She needed to decompress. The events of the day had been tiring, and she knew all of it was because of her and the choices that she had made. Travis now lay in his bed, sleeping off the pain medication that Ashley had given him after she stitched up his head. That head was now almost bald, and even that made her feel awful. Jagger now sat in a jail cell, waiting to see if they could bring Clinton to them. She hated this. She should have made better decisions for everyone involved. The sliding glass door opened, and she looked up, seeing B. The other woman hesitated at the threshold before making her way out into the night.

"Hi," she said to Christine, almost shy.

"Hi," she said back.

It was awkward, and Christine wasn't sure what to do. This woman obviously meant a great deal to Jagger, and she wanted to get to know her too, she just wasn't sure how to do that. The only friend she had made in years was Travis, and that had been based on need and an attraction that she could now no longer deny. B tentatively came over to the all-weather table and had a seat across from her.

They were quiet for a few minutes, until the other woman spoke.

"I've been with Jagger for a while. We're going on a year," she smiled softly. "Well not 'officially', but we've been flirting for at least a year."

Christine wondered what this conversation was going to be, and it made her nervous. Was B going to tell her what an idiot she had been? Was she going to be upset because Jagger now sat in a jail cell, trying to lure out this other man? She didn't want to open her mouth and interrupt, so she kept silent.

"There's been a million times in the last year that he's driven me crazy and I've wanted to kill him," she laughed, before her face turned serious. "But there's been a handful of times since he moved in with me and we've been sleeping in the same bed that he's awoken in the middle of the night. Those nights are bad, he's screaming bloody murder, and sweat is pouring down his body, and he's gasping for breath, and it takes me a long time to calm him down. It always takes him a long time to tell me what causes that. Every time, it's a nightmare about his child-hood, and it's the guilt over leaving you alone. He always tells me that he hoped that by him leaving you alone, you had a better life, but he couldn't shake the feeling that you hadn't. He couldn't shake the feeling that something was wrong with you."

B stopped for a moment, letting those words sink in.

"We were always close," Christine whispered, tears thick in her throat. "I was so mad at him when he left. I couldn't hear the fight that he and my dad had. They were outside, and when Jagger came banging back in the house, up to his room, Dad gave him ten minutes. I remember because I kept watch on that clock as I heard him gathering stuff in his room. I waited at the door of mine, hoping against everything that he would get me and take me with him."

"He wanted to," B interjected. "He's told me that a million times, but you weren't of age, and he knew that your parents would spin it. They would say that he kidnapped you, and then he would be done for. He went back, ya know? A few years ago and then again more recently."

Christine's head shot up. "How recent?"

The other woman cleared her throat and averted her eyes. "Earlier this year, there was a situation. The principal at the school I teach at became obsessed with me. He held me hostage and the Heaven Hill boys, along with Rooster, had to come save me. It brought up a lot of feelings in both Jagger and me. The last thing I remember about being in the room that the principal had me in was that he had me up against the wall, his hand at my throat, he had lifted me so high my feet couldn't touch the ground, and I was having a very hard time breathing. I know I blacked out, but I don't know for how long. Jagger is the one that came in the room and saw it. It apparently triggered something in him about his childhood?" She formed the statement as a question, because it was something she had always wanted to know. Jagger had opened up to her in a big way, but in some cases, he was still very closed off about what he had gone through as a child.

"That was my dad's favorite thing to do," Christine whispered. "He loved to toy with us, and that was an easy way to do it. He would never do it long enough to leave bruises or to make us black out, but he would cut off the circulation long enough so that we would panic. You, of all people, know what it's like to try and breathe and not to be able to. Our dad was an evil man, and our mom was very subservient. She went along with anything he wanted her to."

Hearing her suspicions confirmed made B sad and mad at the same time, but she pushed those feelings back. This wasn't about her; this was about the man that she loved and the woman who would be a part of her life, God willing. "After that ordeal, the both of us began seeing a therapist. Jagger has mentioned some things that happened as a child, but I can tell he's holding back, probably because he doesn't want me to think any less of him—which is dumb, but it's how he is sometimes. One of our sessions a month or so ago, he mentioned you and the guilt that he felt. He told the doctor about having gone back a few years ago and being thrown off the property, but he couldn't shake the feeling that you needed him."

Going back in her mind, she figured that was around the time that she had escaped and Travis had found her. It was crazy how feelings in siblings could be like that. "I did, but luckily around that time is when I met Travis."

Bianca forged on. "The more recent time that he went back to your parents' house, it was abandoned."

That was a huge shock to Christine. Their parents had loved their home. It hadn't been happy, but it had been theirs, and they treated it with the utmost care and respect. "What?"

"Yeah, Jagger wouldn't take me, but according to him,

the yard was grown up and the doors were locked. I'm not sure if he tried to go in or not, but he came back pretty disheartened."

A cold feeling settled over Christine. What if her escaping had meant the end for her parents? She always got the feeling that she was the payment for something. She had never been sure what, but what if her leaving had more consequences than even she knew? "We've gotta get Jagger out of that jail cell. I have a really bad feeling about it," she suddenly had to get him out. "I don't want him there."

"What do you think happened?" B asked, her eyes wide.

"I always got the feeling I was payment for something. It was mentioned in passing a few times. What if my running away meant that payment in full wasn't made? What if Clinton is the reason my parents abandoned their house and he needs payment again? It's obvious from everything I've seen that he has a lot of law enforcement in his pocket. I'm scared that Jagger's there, we've gotta get him out. We need to go about this another way. I won't have him hurt because of me."

"Okay, calm down," Bianca told her, worried that the other woman was going to have a panic attack. "Let's go get Liam, tell him our concerns, and get Rooster to pull him out. It'll be fine."

Christine hoped that it would.

Jagger paced the cell they had placed him in and breathed a sigh. It had been a very long time since he had been in one of these, especially of his own free will. He was pretty sure that had never happened. His thoughts were racing as he paced. He wanted so badly to end this man that had caused such grief for his sister. He also wanted to know exactly what had been done to her and why their dad had given her up so easily. None of it made sense to him, and if he was honest, he was probably in shock. This whole situation was more than he could stand, more than he could process at this point. God, he hoped when he and B had children— and he knew it was going there with her, he loved to see her with Tatum—they wouldn't fuck the kids up.

"Hey, I'm taking you out of here." His head shot up as he heard Rooster come into the area they had him in.

"What? Why?"

"Liam's orders. Apparently Christine and B had a conversation, and neither one of them think you're safe here."

"I can handle myself," Jagger argued.

"I know you can, but apparently what Christine and B talked about was a bit of a game-changer."

That pissed Jagger off beyond words. If the two of them were talking, they should be talking to him so that he knew just what in the fuck was going on. He hated that. "So I'm just gonna leave?"

"I already got the paperwork processed. When this is over I'm gonna have to turn in my fuckin' badge," Rooster said softly.

"Are you kidding or serious?"

Rooster shook his head. "The things I've been doin' are an abuse of power. If I don't hand in my badge, I'm gonna be in so much fuckin' trouble, I'm not gonna be able to get out of it. So yeah, I'm serious. As soon as we find out who Clinton is and what he wants, I'm done here."

Jagger hated to hear that because he knew that for the most part Rooster was good at his job, when he wasn't giving them a hard time. "I'm sorry to hear that. I really am."

Rooster nodded his head and escorted him out into the booking area of the jail so that he could get his stuff back. As they walked out, side by side, they had to stop as a few other inmates were being brought in. A man in a suit standing with the sheriff caught Jagger's eye. He had seen the man before, somewhere. He wasn't sure where, but he could distinctly remember it. The man had a scar on his cheek, not huge, but big enough that you couldn't miss it. And his eyes. They were a startling green color. Jagger knew that before the man lifted his face to look at him. The two of them stared at each other for a long time, until Rooster nudged him.

"I just need you to sign right here."

Jagger did as he was told, standing as close to Rooster as he could. "Find out who that man in the suit is. I know him from somewhere, but I can't place it. I think that might be Clinton."

"You shittin' me?" Rooster breathed, not glancing up at the sheriff and the man but taking note of all the details that he had seen in passing.

"No, I really think that's him."

Rooster took note of the time and handed the piece of paper to Jagger. "Tell Travis to hack into the security cameras and give him this time. Then tell him to run facial recognition on him. That will be the easiest way we can figure out who he is, and if anybody can do it—it's Travis.

He's fuckin' smart."

Jagger took the piece of paper and walked out of the jail, keeping his head straight forward. He could feel the eyes of the man in the suit on him and breathed a sigh of relief when he exited the brick building. There in front were Tyler and Layne. He'd never been so glad to see them in his life, especially when he greeted them, looked around, and saw the suited man walking behind him. It was when he spotted the other two members and watched as Jagger put his cut back on that he went back into the jail.

Chapter Nineteen

Jagger had the decency to wait until the next morning to approach Travis about running the facial recognition. If he were being completely honest, he was nervous. He hadn't meant to attack Travis that way, it was the last thing he had wanted to do. Purposely, he had stayed away until late morning. When he entered the clubhouse, he spotted Tyler.

"You know where Travis is?"

Tyler grimaced. "He and his much shorter hair are in the cave."

"Shorter hair?"

"Yeah, dude. It was kinda short to begin with, but they had to buzz him to put some staples in his head where you busted it wide open. I'm not sure you're the person he wants to see today, if you get what I mean."

Now Jagger felt really bad. His temper had gotten the better of him—that and the shock. "Has Liam said anything?" Things like that could have more than one potential consequence. It normally was not kosher to fight in the clubhouse.

"Nah, I think he gets it. Hell, we all get it, but the rest of us are far enough away from the situation to understand that he was doing what he thought was right. At the same time, we all understand just how pissed you are. Nobody here was right, but it's not clear if anyone was wrong either."

This was a no-win situation. Both Jagger and Christine were products of people who should never have been parents to begin with. They were caught in the middle of something that wasn't even of their own making. Now they had to figure out how they were going to live their own lives. It was up to them to determine if they wanted to continue the cycle of abuse or make a different choice. Jagger knew what he wanted to do, but that would include fixing things with both Travis and Christine. He had flown off the handle first and asked questions later, something that he had previously been working on. "I know, I'm gonna go talk to him. I need him to run a facial recognition on someone anyway."

"Good luck, dude. He may not be ready to see you," Tyler smiled over his skull mug. "You wanna rub the mug for luck?"

"Fuck you," Jagger chuckled.

Travis' head hurt like a bitch, but Ashley, the club's doctor, had assured him the concussion wasn't bad, but it was going to be painful. He reached up and ran his hand over the buzz cut he now had and frowned. He'd never been one of the guys that cared to have long hair, but he'd liked to have enough that he could brush. This was just short of being bald, and he wasn't sure how he felt about it. At twenty-four, was it unusual to wonder if it would come back? Sighing, he went back to checking his bank of cameras. This was where he felt the best, in front of his electronics. It had been too long since he had sat here and done this. He knew that if he wanted to stop feeling off-kilter, he was going to have to do it more often. Just as he was getting involved in the things he needed to do, there was a knock on the doorframe. He looked up, expecting to see Liam or Tyler. When he saw Jagger there, he immediately stuck up a middle finger.

"What the fuck are you doing here?

Jagger took offense, and even though he knew it wasn't the best thing, to be an ass, he answered. "Same as what you're doing here. I wear the same patch on my back, fucker."

"I understand that you're pissed at me, but right now I'm fuckin' pissed at you. They cut my hair, I had to get staples, I have a concussion, and my head is killing me. If you could tell me what you want and then leave me the hell alone, I think we would both be better off." Travis was usually the quietest in the club, but sometimes he had to let his feelings be known, and this was one of those times.

Jagger inhaled deeply. "I'm sorry, I shouldn't have said that."

Travis didn't know if he could accept the apology. It wasn't in him to forgive easily because it took him a long time to get to the point that he was that pissed at someone. "You shouldn't have."

"But you shouldn't have kept my sister from me either."

That flat-out pissed Travis off. "You act like I'm the

man who held her against her will. I hate to break it to you, Jagger, but I didn't keep her from you. She kept herself from you. She didn't want you to know, she didn't want to see you. I've done the best I can with her, trying to convince her that she needed to tell you that she was alive, tell you what happened in her life, but she wouldn't or couldn't. I felt like a bastard every time I left here to go see her, and then when I came back—every time, I wanted to tell you where I had been. She didn't want that. The relationship I had with her was so shaky—fuck, she was so shaky—I was afraid to break her confidence. It was obvious that so many people had already done that and that she would not hesitate to run. I don't have to fuckin' explain myself to you, asshole."

"She didn't want to see me?"

Maybe that blow had been a little harsh. "She didn't want to see anybody," he amended. "I still don't know everything that happened to her, Jagger, but I think she was treated like a human slave. I think she blamed, or blames, you in a way. That's something the two of you are going to have to work out, and I refuse to be stuck in the middle of it. I did what I thought was best. If you don't agree with that, then get the fuck over it. What do you want?"

Jagger had to accept that Travis needed some more time before he was ready to forgive and move on. "There was a man at the jail last night. Both Rooster and I think it was Clinton. I have a time that you need to hack into the security cameras at the jail. Rooster said to run facial recognition on him."

"Glad I'm taking orders from Rooster now," he mumbled under his breath.

"I know you're pissed at me, just like I'm pissed at you, but we both want the same thing. To help Christine put this behind her. Can we at least work together?"

That made Travis feel like shit. They were both working towards the same goal, and they needed to do that by being mature adults. Travis sighed. "We can, because more than anything I want her to be free, and with that freedom, I want her to choose to stay here. Believe me, there's something in me that wonders if she's staying here just because I saved her. If she's given the option of going anywhere she wants, there's a part of me that thinks she's going to leave."

"Neither one of us want that."

"No, we don't, so we have to figure this all out and then hope she doesn't get sick of us and leave in the middle of the night."

They both sat there in silence as Travis started doing what he did best. Jagger wouldn't even know where to begin, but with a few clicks on a computer screen and a keyboard, Travis was into the mainframe of the sheriff's office. Jagger watched as Travis reached over and grabbed a sucker out of his candy stash. It was such a habit for him; he didn't even look as he unwrapped the sucker, threw away the packaging in the trash, and then stuck the candy in his mouth. Jagger shook his head, a grin on his face.

"What time did Rooster want me to look at?"

Jagger looked down at the piece of paper that he held in his hands, giving him the time. He watched as Jagger pulled up another program, imported something into it, and then clicked a button. After he clicked the button, he sat back.

"Now we just gotta wait. It shouldn't take long though. I already did a little research on this guy myself, but something about him never sat right with me."

"What's that?" Jagger asked, sitting in the seat, his chin propped on his hand. This was the most boring shit in the world to him.

"How did he come into contact with young women? Christine told me that there were a few more when she first came to live there. They disappeared towards the end, but they started out there. What did he do, where did he come into contact with them?"

Jagger flashed back to his own childhood, the church camp where he'd almost been violated. The summer that had changed his life forever. "You'd be surprised. They have camps, and if you have zealot parents, like we did, they will send you anywhere to help save your soul."

"I just don't understand this whole arranged marriage thing. What did your parents hope to get by doing it?"

And that was it, it was hard to explain to someone who hadn't grown up the way they had. Until they had become a certain age, neither one of them had really understood just how weird their lives were, but by then they were used to it and there was no turning back.

"Because, when all your parents care about is being the perfect church members, they will do anything. I'm sure this man came to my parents, told them that he could make them look better in the eyes of the church, probably offered them some money, and they signed on the dotted line. When all you want to do is look good for other people, it doesn't seem to matter what you do to accomplish that. Our parents alienated two children, and neither one of us know what's actually happened to them, but I have a bad feeling that they learned just how shitty it can be to care that much what others think of you." He didn't want to add that it had possibly all been put in motion because he'd refused to let himself be touched as a teenager, not unless he had to.

The whole thing was crazy to Travis. He wasn't close to his mom, his parents had never been married, and he didn't have a relationship with his father to speak of, but he knew that if he ever needed anything he could call his mom. She wouldn't come running, but she would be there. She knew what he did, who he was, and why he had chosen this path in his life. She didn't necessarily agree with it, but she had never turned her back on him and she had never tried to sabotage his life.

"I can't imagine living in that house."

Jagger blew out a deep breath. "It wasn't easy. Our dad wasn't the type of man to yell. He was the type of man to beat first and talk later. That's why I feel awful about your head," Jagger apologized. "I was just like him in that moment, even though I promised myself I never would be. I told myself my whole life that I would find out the situation before reacting, and it took two minutes for me to revert to the way he was. Throw fists first and ask questions later. I'm really ashamed of that Travis, and I'm sorry that you were on the receiving end of that."

"Dude, my head hurts, and I'm still pissed, but I can tell you right now, you are not one damn ounce like your daddy. It came from a good place, not an evil place. If I had a sister, I would have done the same thing. I understand it, and I don't hold it against you. I just gotta get over the fact that my head hurts," Travis grinned.

Jagger opened his mouth to say something else, but right then the computer dinged that it had a match. When the two of them turned their eyes back to the screen, Jagger's blood ran cold. He knew this man.

Chapter Twenty

"How do you know him?" Travis asked as he started to pull up all the pertinent information that he needed. Some of it was in his original report on the man, but now that he had the facial recognition, it looked like he went by at least two other aliases as well.

The laugh that came was dry and hollow. "He approached me as a teenager, tried to get into my pants."

"What?"

He hated telling other people about this. Even though he knew that it wasn't his fault, he still felt shame. He knew that he shouldn't, but even after months of talking to Doc Jones about it, it still gave him a little anxiety. "Yeah, he was an elder and a pastor in the sector of our church. He got a young girl pregnant, and then he tried to get into my pants. It's what made me turn my back on religion. I didn't know him as Clinton Herrington though, so obviously he used one of those aliases with us."

Travis pushed a few more keys. "So we've got a guy with a serial pattern, who liked to prey on young kids?"

"Exactly."

It was all beginning to click in his mind and his fingers

flew on the keyboard. "And after some of the stuff that Christy told me, I'm thinking he's got a graveyard on that property."

Jagger's mind was working a million miles a minute. "You think we can get in there?"

"I think we can get in." Travis nodded as he pulled up some images on his screen and made notes on a piece of paper. "The problem is gonna be finding anything. We need our hands on the kind of equipment that we normally can't get our hands on, but I know somebody who can. It will also depend on how long he's been doing this, and how well he is at covering his tracks."

"Who?"

Travis sighed. "Rooster."

"You're his family, you call him."

It was hard to explain to people who weren't his blood family the relationship there. It had never been what one would call loving, but they had for the most part gotten along until Travis decided to go outlaw and Rooster decided to be the law. Travis, however, could see things changing with his cousin. In the past two years, he'd loosened the grip he held on himself, started helping the club a lot more than any of them cared to admit, and he no longer walked like he had a stick up his ass. "I'll ask him, but it might be better if we get Liam to ask him."

"No, this has gotta come from you. I think it'll mean more if it comes from you. I think he wants that relationship with you again."

"Fine." He jerked his cell phone off the table where it sat beside him and dialed the number. He firmly expected it to go to voicemail, but Rooster picked up on the first ring.

"Yeah, is everything alright?" Worry was evident in his voice, but Travis had to admit, it'd been a long time since he'd called him out of the blue.

"Everything's fine. I have a favor."

"I'll do what I can to help," he offered.

Travis went on to explain their situation and their suspicions. When he was done, Rooster whistled through his teeth. "Goddamn, this could be big."

"It could be, but we need that equipment to see what's there, and we need an open window. We don't need other law enforcement to be out there. I've looked at everything I can online. He's got a fortress out there, almost like he expects the ATF to come knockin' on his door one day."

Rooster was walking as he talked. "Sorry, I was around some people I didn't want to hear this conversation. I can get you the equipment that you need tonight, and I can try to keep people away, but there's this new asshole here."

"The guy that's been breaking up the drag races and who chased us the other day?"

"Yeah, he's got a hard-on for anything illegal in this town."

Travis couldn't help it. "Just like you used to."

"Worse," Rooster laughed. "I can get you what you need, but you gotta be quick. I need it back by tomorrow morning, and you're gonna need to clean it for me. I don't know how, it has internal hard drives and all that bullshit."

"I'll take care of it, you get us what we need."

Later on that night, Travis was suiting up, wearing what he normally wore when they did break-ins, and he'd been careful not to mention anything to Christine. He didn't want to explain what was happening because he didn't want to bring up bad memories for her. At least not until they knew exactly what they were working with. He slipped a bulletproof vest over his shirt.

"Why are you wearing that?" she asked, her eyes wide.

"For protection," he answered casually.

"Protection from what?" This was the first time she'd been around when he had been doing something for the club, and she wasn't used to this, but if she was going to stay here, she was going to have to get used to it.

"Your first rule as a woman here. Don't ask questions about where we go at night wearing bulletproof vests. We can't answer that, for your protection and ours. Sometimes what we do could get you in trouble, and if someone was to ask you where I was going and you say you don't know, I want that to be the damn truth."

The words that came out of his mouth pissed her off, but then she saw him reach into a cabinet and pull out a handgun. "You think you're gonna need that?" she asked quietly.

"You never know. When we go on jobs, it can sometimes get dicey. It's either kill or be killed; we have to protect ourselves," he answered truthfully. "Is this scaring you?"

"No." She shook her head. "I've never seen this side of you, and it's different."

"It's all a part of who I am," he reminded her, putting on his boots and slipping a KBAR inside. "I've never hidden from you what I do, but I've never exactly told you about it either."

"I'm not an idiot or deaf," she deadpanned. "I hear things all the time in this town, and I even hear you talk. I just chose not to ask questions, and if you don't want me to ask those questions, I won't. I understand that sometimes you can't talk about what you do."

Well that was a lot easier than he assumed it would be. "I'll be back in a little while. Don't wait up in case we're late, this could take a while."

She nodded before walking over to him and slipping her arms around his neck, pulling him closer to her. "Be careful." She kissed him on the cheek. "When you're done, text me at least, in case I'm still awake."

"I will," he promised, tangling his hands in her hair and bringing her mouth to his. He hated that he couldn't tell he where they were going and what they were looking for. This was going to hurt her if their suspicions were correct, but part of this was to help her. If that guy was what they all thought, a serial killer, then she could finally be free of him. If she was free of him, then the two of them could live their lives without fear, and he wanted that. He kissed her one more time before walking out of the dorm room and making his way towards the garage.

"Jagger's on his way," Liam told Travis as he entered the garage. "There was a wreck on Covington, and he got stuck."

Travis nodded. "You sure you wanna come with us?"

"Yeah, Rooster's gone out of his way to help us this time. I feel like I need to be there. He didn't have to okay the use of that equipment; he put himself out there for this. I feel like, too, I should be there just in case this guy comes out and you and Jagger want to kill him. I don't want anybody to get in the type of situation that we can't get out of, and I'm in charge of how the two of you act. Keep your shit together, no matter what we see here."

"I get what you're saying and I appreciate it. Believe it or not, I'm glad you're coming, for all of the reasons that you just mentioned."

They were quiet while they readied their bikes. It was colder than normal for late fall, early winter. Because of that, Travis pulled a knit hat over his almost bald held and then pulled the hood of the sweatshirt he also wore over it. "Not used to the almost baldness," he laughed.

Liam grinned right back at him. "Dude, that sucked, but you're rockin' it, ya know? It looks good."

"You're just sayin' that 'cause you don't want me to be pissed at Jagger for it anymore. I'm not, really. I did deserve it, but I would have preferred not to have staples put in the back of my head. And I would really have liked to keep my hair."

The loud rumble of a motorcycle sounded as they talked. "Speak of the devil and he shall appear," Liam joked.

They could hear Jagger park in front of the garage and enter it. They both looked up and laughed. He had on a face mask that looked like a skull. "Y'all like it? It's new. B said she was sick of me wearin' that damn bandana. I think this one's pretty badass!"

Travis had missed this, the brotherhood. Before they went to do something they knew they weren't supposed to, there were always a ton of jokes, a lot of trying to release the tension by just being stupid. He missed this, and he was so thankful they were getting it right now.

"That is pretty badass," Liam agreed, slapping Jagger on the back.

"Is it as cold as it feels?" Travis asked.

"Yeah, you want something in front of your face. Wind is a little high tonight."

That sucked for some of the equipment they were going to use, but he had anything with a battery strapped to his skin to keep it warm. They would be fine, he told himself. Pulling out his own bandana, he wrapped it around his face and then put his helmet on.

"We ready?" Liam asked the two of them.

"As I'll ever be," Travis admitted.

None of them were looking forward to what they knew they might find, but they all knew it was a necessary evil. For some of them, this would help them move on with their lives; for the rest of them, it meant that Heaven Hill was getting back into the game. They had been quiet for too long. It was time to let the people of the town and surrounding counties that they wouldn't stand for this kind of shit anymore. All three of them started their bikes and within moments were driving down the gravel of the driveway and turning onto Porter Pike. A few miles down the road, a sheriff car pulled in front of them and flashed his lights—they recognized it as Rooster's car. He escorted them to the county line. Once they made it to Simpson County, he dropped off, giving them a honk and a wave. It didn't escape Travis' notice that he did a U-turn on the interstate and parked on the north bound side. He was waiting for them to come back. That meant more to him than he cared to examine, but right now, it was time to get to work.

Chapter Twenty-One

It hadn't been easy getting behind the electrified barbed wire fence that surrounded the property, but they had managed it. Took them over an hour, and they knew at this point they had no time to lose. It was a struggle they hadn't counted on.

"You sure you know how to work this stuff?" Liam asked Travis as he laid everything out and began putting batteries in the pieces that needed it.

"I'm not a dumbass. I set up your phone and everything having to deal with that. Might I also add, I make sure every single one of our houses is safe. I know what I'm doing, I just need to make sure I do it right. These batteries don't last forever, and we need a little juice to figure out what works best."

Jagger kept watch towards the main house, watching through a pair of binoculars for anything that could be taken as a threat from the man who lived there. "Everything's quiet up this way. Just do what you need to. I'll let ya know if we've got to book it."

Liam wished he could be of some help to Travis, but he knew that if he tried, he would only help in fucking everything up. "If you need me to do something, let me know."

Travis nodded and began messing with the keys on the small laptop he'd brought with him. Without a thought, Travis reached into his pocket, took out a piece of hard candy, unwrapped it, and popped it into his mouth.

"You really can't concentrate without that, can you?" Liam chuckled, blowing his breath into his hands.

"It's either that or die of lung cancer. I gotta do something while I'm concentrating, and my smokin' was gettin' out of hand. Tyler makes fun of the ten pounds I've put on, but at least I'm not waking up in the morning hacking my lungs out. I'm still smoking, just not as much."

There wasn't much to argue about to that. Travis did have a point. Liam decided instead that he should probably shut his mouth. It was very quiet this time of night. The only thing they could hear was the wind howling, and Liam threw up a silent prayer that everything went off without a hitch so that they could be back before the sun rose.

"Here, take this," Travis held something out to him that looked like a metal detector. "Walk in a slow line and move that out in front of you. It's gonna map the ground below. If there's something underneath there, it'll show it in startling detail on this laptop."

Grateful for something to do, Liam did as he was told. "How far do you want me to walk it?" He asked Travis.

"Keep going, I'll tell you when to stop."

He walked for what felt like hours, and when he looked up, Liam was concerned with how close he'd gotten to the house.

"Stop," Travis told him.

Liam turned; something about the tone of Travis' voice

gave him pause. When he looked back, Travis was white as a ghost, and he wasn't even working on the candy he had in his mouth. "You alright? It's not your head is it?"

"No, it's what's on this screen. I want you two to come here and look, make sure what I think I'm seein' is what I'm seein'."

Liam shut off the equipment, and Jagger flipped the binoculars from his eyes as they both made their way over to where he sat. Travis turned the laptop around and waited for their reactions. Liam wasn't sure what he was looking at, but he if he looked close enough, he thought he saw a skeleton. "Are those bones?"

Liam shivered, more pissed than he had ever been in his life. "Grab that shit up; let's get the fuck outta here. We're going to make sure, no matter what we have to do, that this asshole is taken care of. We need to get this to Rooster, explain to him where it's at, and for once let the authorities handle this. This man is sick, serial killer sick. I don't want him to find us here. Let's go." Not much made Liam scared, but he did not want this man to know they were on the property. There was no telling what he would do, and tonight wasn't the night that he wanted to die.

Both Travis and Jagger nodded their heads. They had never felt so strongly about something in their lives.

Rooster felt his stomach clench and roll as he looked at the information that Jagger, Travis, and Liam had brought back to him. "Are we sure this is for real? If I pull the trigger on this and we come to find out that it's not, we're looking at a lot of backlash."

Liam nodded. "I saw it with my own two eyes. Unfortunately, it's all real. That imaging equipment you got your hands on for us—there are a lot of unmarked graves on that property. He's been doing this a long time. Christine's lucky she got out when she did."

"Fuck," Rooster breathed. "I can't take this to my superiors, they'll cover it up. They've obviously been covering for him for a very long time."

Liam glanced over at his friend. "Tyler, do you think Meredith still has some of her contacts at the news station? If they break the story and notify the state police, the state police will have to notify the Feds. That means we can completely bypass city and county jurisdiction."

"Let me text her and see what she says." Tyler pulled his phone out of his pants pocket and went to work.

"It was bad?" Rooster asked Liam.

"Yeah, it's all on the backside of the property—what you can't see from the road. I've never seen anything like it." Liam swallowed hard.

Rooster had nothing to say. The images and pictures they had brought to him said enough.

"Those graves are shallow too. They have to be for that imaging equipment to pick it up. That's why I know he thinks he's invincible. If he was worried about it, there would be no way we could find it. You feel me?"

Rooster nodded his head, whistling through his teeth. He had never seen anything like this, and he knew it would rock the small Franklin community as well as the surrounding ones. "He's a collector, he collects bodies."

"Very much so. I can't tell you when the last person

was buried there, I'm not a forensic person, but I would be willing to bet that the last person Christine saw alive there is the freshest grave. For some reason, he liked her; he wasn't going to get rid of her. After seeing the haphazard way he left all these, there was a reason he kept her in that house."

Rooster chewed on the end of his pen. "There's some other reason he kept Christine, other than the fact she was his favorite. He was waiting on something, she hadn't triggered him yet."

The room was quiet as they thought.

Liam shook his head. "You know I've done and seen some crazy shit. I've killed men, you know this. I draw the line at intentionally hurting a woman—unless she's trying to kill me. If it's me protecting myself, it's completely different. It's like a cult, man, seriously. You're going to have to talk to Christine. Maybe she knows more and she just doesn't realize how important it is. She's lucky that she got out when she did."

"Can I have both her and Meredith in here? I think if Meredith hears the story, then she's going to be more apt to help us out. I'm also kind of thinking maybe Christine wasn't completely honest with Jagger and Travis, maybe because she's ashamed."

Liam let out a deep breath. "I see where you're coming from. I'll go grab them, and then I'm going home and hugging the shit out of Mandy and Tatum and promising to every god that I can find that they will never have to fuckin' live that way."

Rooster glanced over to where Tyler sat. "I know you want to be here for Meredith, but I don't think Christine is going to talk with you in here."

The big man pushed himself off the wall and strode over to where Rooster sat. "Liam and Travis seem to have accepted you, and that means a lot to me." He pushed back a lock of his hair that had fallen in his face. "But Meredith is my responsibility. I will wait outside that door, and if I even get the feeling you're harassing her, I don't give a fuck if you are a sheriff or what you've done in the past to help us—I will hurt you."

"I wouldn't expect anything less from you, Tyler. I promise, she's in good hands."

When Tyler left, Rooster took a deep breath. This was going to play out only one way. He was going to have to give the information to the proper authorities, and then he was going to have to hand in his resignation. He was too far in now, and if he was honest, his heart was no longer in law enforcement. Pulling his cell phone out of his pocket, he glanced at the picture that was the lock screen and had to admit that because of the woman who decorated it, his heart was now a lot more outlaw. The thought didn't even give him the anxiety that he knew it once would have. For Roni he would do whatever it took.

"I want to thank the two of you for coming to see me."

Meredith laughed softly from where she sat. "Like we had any choice, Rooster, but I know that my big, bad husband is right outside the door. I know you aren't going to be stupid like that."

Christine sat beside her, picking at her fingernails. "I'm

not sure what you want with me," she said softly.

Rooster was glad to have Meredith with him. He, like the rest of them, knew what had happened to her, and he had a feeling that some of the same things had happened with Christine. He wasn't sure at all how to approach this, so he did it with as much caution as he could. "I don't think you lied to Travis and Jagger about what happened to you at Clinton's house, but I think you withheld some information. I also think that you knew some things were happening, but you weren't sure what they were. I need your help."

"I don't know how I can help you," she argued.

He pulled one of the pictures out of the packet that the boys had provided him with. "Some of the guys went onto the property today to do some surveillance on him. We want you free, we don't want you to have to worry if he's going to come back and find you. We want you to live your life in peace," he explained. "When they got there they found a dozen shallow graves with what looked like women in them."

Her face was stone cold until he mentioned the women, and then it cracked and her shoulders heaved, sobs tearing from her throat.

Meredith quickly put her arms around the other woman. "Jesus, Rooster! Couldn't you have eased into that?"

Did this woman really think there was a way to ease into the fact that they had found shallow graves on a farm in Simpson County? "Really? No matter how you slice this, it's awful, sick, and twisted. You can't spin this, reporter."

"I knew something was going on, but I didn't know what. They just disappeared, after they got pregnant."

Christine whispered.

"Did you know for sure they were pregnant?" Rooster questioned, softly. That was a fact they hadn't known about, but it would make sense.

"There were all the signs." She shook her head. "But I didn't know for sure, it's not like we ever had a doctor come see us."

"Is there a reason why you never became pregnant?" Rooster asked as gently as possible.

She diverted her eyes. "I did things, things I always heard were old wives' tales, but I counted on them. They worked," she laughed harshly. "I don't know if it's because of what I did, or if maybe I just can't have children. Thank God that I never had to deal with what the rest of them had to deal with."

"Did you ever see him hurt any of the women?"

Tears sprang to her eyes, and her throat started to close. "He hurt all of us in some way—whether it be mentally or physically. He backhanded me a few times, so there's nothing I don't think he didn't do."

"So it would be within the realm of possibility that he killed these women?" Rooster finished for her.

"I heard him once, arguing with someone. I'm not sure who it was, but the other person was telling him that he was going to have to stop. There were only so many women that could go missing in the community before people became suspicious, and he wasn't sure he could get him out of it anymore." She told him about the cats dying one by one and the bloody towels.

Rooster had a sinking feeling that person had been someone at the sheriff's office, hiding this whole thing. "I just want you to know that they aren't going to mention your name. I'm taking all this information to the FBI as soon as I leave here, but your name will be left out of this."

"We're married," she cried. "How is my name going to be kept out of this? I want a divorce; I don't want to have anything to do with him anymore."

"You leave all of that to me."

Meredith had kept quiet throughout the exchange. "I'm so sorry for everything that you've been through Christine. There's a part of me that understands some of what you've gone through. I was raped in the past. I've been working for over the past year to get beyond it. I know a great person that you can talk to—if that's something that you need."

Christine looked at the other woman. "I appreciate that. Right now, I'm not sure what I want to do, but I will keep it in mind."

"Can you help me get this to the people I need to get it to?" Rooster asked Meredith. "I don't want this intercepted before I have a chance to get it people who aren't being paid off."

She nodded. "I know exactly who you need to talk to. After the bank robberies and the disappearance of Raymond Tucker, the FBI sat up a field office here. I just so happen to know the special agent in charge. Don't ask how I became chummy with him, but I can get you where you need to be. Give me until tomorrow morning and let me take a few pictures of the information you have."

If there was one thing Rooster knew, it was that Meredith was capable of almost anything; he'd seen it numerous times. She would be an invaluable friend to have, and he was glad she was on their side. It didn't escape him that he was already thinking of himself as a member of the Heaven Hill MC; even if that wasn't an idea he had entertained for a long time. Things were about to change, and it was time. He wasn't the same man he'd been years ago—the job had worn on him, and he was now ready for something new, something different. As soon as he wrapped up giving this information to who needed it and covering his ass, he was gone. He hadn't felt this free in a long time, and he knew part of that was because of the visit he had paid to Roni. He was ready to give this part of his life another chance—provided that he and Liam could work through their own bullshit.

Times were definitely changing.

Chapter Twenty-Two

"You saw it?" Christine asked Travis as she made her way into the room the two of them called their own. "You saw the graveyard?"

He nodded. "That was something of the freakiest shit I have ever seen in my life. The fact that someone could kill for what seemed like sport, to me, is insane. Granted, we've done some things as an MC that I think people might look down upon, but we've never done it for the fun of it."

"I think I know why he did it," she told him, swallowing roughly.

"I don't know if I want to hear," he admitted. Walking over to where she stood, he put his arms around her neck and pulled to him.

She held on for dear life, wrapping her arms around his waist. "I think he saw them as a sacrifice, you know, to God, and that since he was doubly sacrificing, then he would be more heavily favored. I know it sounds weird, but if you could hear him sometimes," she covered her ears. "He would chant, and those chants had to do with offerings, and it was always after that another woman would disappear."

He wanted to take this away from her, show her that this was such a skewed version of life. "I promise you, Christy. This is not how life really is; it's not how it's supposed to be."

"Will I be happy with you?" she whispered against the tears in her eyes.

"You will. I will live every day of my life proving to you that I'm good enough, that I will never do anything to hurt you intentionally. I'm not going to promise to never hurt you, because we both know that love hurts. It's just a fact of life."

"Is that what this is? Love?" she asked him, scared to say those words.

He crowded her, pushing her back against the door, and put his hands at her neck, tilting her chin up. It forced her eyes to meet his. "I think so," he grinned. It was crooked and so endearing that she had to grin back.

"I think so too," she whispered. "But I am so fucking scared, Travis, so scared."

"Haven't I proven to you how serious I am?" He was careful to keep his tone level, to not make any overtures that she would see as threatening.

She thought back to everything he had done for her. He'd kept her secret when he hadn't had to, he'd gotten her a job, a house, a dependable car, and then when all of that had been threatened, he'd moved her into his dorm room. All the while, he'd lied to her brother and everyone else in the clubhouse to help her feel safe. Then he'd gone to the place that had been the scariest for her, with Liam and her brother; he had broken into Clinton's property and gotten the information that would send the man to jail. He had set her free. That may not have been what he set out to do back six months ago when they had first met, but he'd given her everything.

"You have. You've gone above and beyond the call of duty. I am so damn lucky to have you. I'm lucky that you've been there at every turn, especially when this all got to be insane. I'm lucky you've slept by me every night since I got here, and I'm so lucky that you still believe in me."

"I do," he agreed. "I believe that you can be and do any damn thing you wanna do. Clinton Herrington may have ruined one part of your life, but he didn't ruin the whole thing. Don't let him. We have our whole lives ahead of us. What you've endured has been more than anyone should have to endure in their whole lifetime, but you've gotten it out of the way. It won't always be smooth sailing, but as long as we're together, I want to live it."

"I do too." She smiled up at him.

It was that smile that made him feel like he'd won the lottery and that he was the luckiest man in the world. Unable to hold back this time, he bent his head forward, capturing her lips with his. He reached up, tangling his hands in her hair, tilting her head back. With her neck exposed, he got busy, licking, sucking, biting, any patch of skin that he could get to. She sighed, wrapping her arms around his neck. He slid his hands down her back, picking her up against him, and walked them over to the bed.

"Promise me," she told him, ripping her mouth from his. "Promise me that I'm not going to wake up tomorrow and this has all been some kind of crazy dream."

"It's not, I swear to you." He shoved his cut off, his shirt over his body, and then went to work on her clothes.

Looking back, Christine wouldn't be able to tell anyone how it happened. How she ended up with her back against the mattress, his body pressing hers against it, she didn't know. All she knew was that she loved the feel of his body covering hers. At one point this would have caused her a lot of anxiety. It always had with Clinton, but she loved this, she loved when Travis lay over top of her so that every inch of his body covered hers. She didn't know where she ended and he began.

"You okay?" he asked, his lips trailing down her throat as he grasped her hands and held them up above her head, twining their fingers together.

She smiled, moaning when he slipped inside her body. "Perfect."

He didn't miss the tears that came to her eyes. "You sure?"

"Yeah." The shake of her head was watery, and those tears spilled against her cheeks. "Never thought I'd be here, never thought I'd feel so free."

Travis understood everything that she said, and he knew the emotions running through her were strong. He buried his lips into her neck as he canted a rhythm into her body. She was right—everything about this was perfect. He knew he would never be able to have this with anyone besides her. He had never wanted it with anyone besides her and knew that he never would. His thrust increased when her legs wrapped around his waist. He could feel her getting softer, feel her accepting him more. Her heels dug into his back, and she moaned loudly, straining against his hands.

"Feel good?" he asked, his mouth near her ear.

She took a deep breath, nodding, hissing when his teeth captured her earlobe. Reluctantly, he let go of one of her hands and ran it down her cheek and neck, tilting her just as he liked her. There, he captured her lips with his, his tongue stroking against hers. He knew that she was into it when the free hand left the mattress and tried to bury in his now non-existent hair. Instead, she moved it down to his neck and curled her fingers around the side, holding him as closely to her as she could. Travis let himself go, pushing his hips deep into her body and then pulling out with the frantic pace. The hand he'd had at her neck trailed down her body until it go to her core. He moaned into her mouth, ripping their lips apart as he felt the wetness there.

"Fuck, Christine," he rasped.

"It's you, all you," she breathed against him. She tilted her hips up, knowing that he would finish her off before she could even give voice to the question. She trusted him with every ounce of herself, completely trusted him. She had never been able to say that about another human being before, and she loved that she could say it about him.

His fingers that were entwined with hers griped tightly, and his head buried back in her neck as he gasped, grunting loudly against the hot skin there. There was something about the quiet way he let go of himself that she loved, that always pushed her over the edge. Their heavy breathing mingled with one another, and they lazily moved against each other until they came to a slow stop. It was peacefully quiet between the two of them, and she sighed deeply, knowing this was exactly where she wanted to be, knowing this was exactly who she wanted to be with.

Meredith hung up her phone, glancing at the three men who faced her. If she were a lesser woman, the three sets of eyes that were Rooster, Liam, and her own husband would have made her cower. But this, this was her area of expertise, and even though she didn't do it as a job anymore, she loved when she got to play. "We need to drop it off at News Center tonight. The field officer is going to meet us there. He'll have his team, and once they view it and deem it worthy, they'll be paying Clinton a visit before the end of the night."

"Can we tag along?" Liam asked Rooster.

Usually Rooster would say no, but since he knew this was the last job he was going to pull for the sheriff's department, he shrugged. "Whatever you wanna do. Just remember that after tonight I won't be able to do any of you any favors. Make sure Jagger and Travis stay under control, if they do go."

Liam wanted to question his old friend about what he meant by not being able to do them any favors after tonight, Jagger had mentioned that Rooster was feeling stifled. There had been a weird sense about him for the past few days, almost like he had made decisions that he didn't want to discuss. "You leavin' the force?"

"I think we're gonna need to talk, but I don't want it to be here, and I don't want it to be now."

That made Liam uneasy, but he agreed, mostly because of everything that Rooster had done to help them out. He couldn't keep asking without giving something in return. Every relationship had to have the perfect combination of give and take—and he was getting nervous that he was only taking from Rooster lately.

"Alright, so we're heading out there?" Tyler asked.

"We are," Meredith nodded. "I'm gonna throw this out there, I don't think we should tell Jagger and Travis where we're going or what we're doing. There's too much going on, and they are both way too close to the whole situation. That's the last thing Christine needs—to see her brother or boyfriend get hauled off in handcuffs for trying to kill her husband. Let's just go get this over and done with, then we can come back and tell everybody the outcome."

Liam rolled that around in his head for a few minutes. He knew that what Meredith said was right and that it would be what was best for the club, not just for a few people. "Sounds like a plan. Let's go get this over with."

He made his way out to his bike, watching Rooster as he did. He wasn't stupid; he knew what was going on, and he knew that after this was over Rooster was going to come to them and want to be a part of the club. That wasn't as surprising as it had been at one time, and he would welcome his once best friend back with open arms. The plans he had for the club from here on out would benefit from any and everything that Rooster could bring to them. He was sick of saving damsels in distress, he was sick of putting his family in danger—they were going back to what they knew after this was all over. Working at the shop and runs at night. He was sick of sleeping with one eye open, worried that some freak would come in the middle of the night and slaughter them all. It was a false sense of security, Liam knew that, but he also knew where he was comfortable. Comfortable for him was on the back of a bike, not trying to keep his guys from imploding. That part was over.

Chapter Twenty-Three

Meredith could feel Tyler's gaze on her back as she met with one of her former co-workers and the field agent of the FBI in charge of the Bowling Green area. She could tell just by the way she felt that he was twitchy, that he didn't like her being around all this law enforcement, but she knew that Clinton was much bigger fish than Heaven Hill had ever been for them. Religious zealots were a dime a dozen, but the Feds always looked good in the public eye when they could bring a group of them down. Waco being the perfect example. They would gladly tout the America experience and get patriotic, and then they would look like the best people in the world. For a few days, even the conspiracy theorists would put their trust in the government. She knew that as soon as she called her contact with this information, they would call in for a full-scale operation.

She smiled slightly at her husband as she walked over to where he stood. "They're about to give us some bulletproof vests, and it's okay for us to ride along, as long as we stay at the periphery."

He was proud of her, proud that she was so willing to help other people, willing to sacrifice the life she had etched out for herself after her rapist had taken away a part of her life. It was getting chilly now that they were moving into November, so he put his big hands on her cheeks to try and get some of the redness out. "You stay behind me, no matter what."

"I will always trust you to protect me, I promise you that."

Rooster walked over, Liam in tow. "I just got a call that they've raided the sheriff's offices in three counties, and they've arrested those same three sheriffs."

"You think those are the ones that were working with Clinton?" Tyler asked, his eyebrow raised.

"Pretty positive," Rooster nodded. "They're going to get rid of anyone who can tamper with evidence before they go get him. The amount of bodies you all found on his property—this is going to be huge. I have a feeling they're going to find Jagger and Christine's parents amongst the dead."

Nobody else had said those words, but Meredith had thought it too. "I figured too, especially when B mentioned that Jagger had been back and their house was abandoned. I have a feeling that when a person ceased being an asset to him, he got rid of them any way he could."

"Meredith!"

Her head whipped around as she heard her voice called. It was her old co-worker. "We're heading out."

She nodded, and the group of them walked over to where the bikes sat, each of them putting on the bullet-proof vests. It was quiet as they got dressed, ready for battle, even though this wasn't their battle this time. They followed the convoy along, none of them really sure what they would face when they got there.

Christine was deep in a cocoon of warmness. Her body was comfortable, and she could feel strong arms around her. The only thing invading the peacefulness was a loud knock at the door.

"Ignore them, they'll go away," a deep voice against her ear said. That voice was scratchy with the sound of sleep and caused goose bumps to form on her arms. She loved when she could hear him like that. It meant even more now that he had told her how he felt about her.

A few minutes later, it was obvious that the other person was not going to go away. Finally the two of them got up, both covering themselves minimally as Travis made his way to the door. "What the fuck do you want?" he asked as he slung the door open. He took a step back when he saw Rooster standing there, a stark look on his face. "What?"

"I need to talk to Christine," he told Travis.

"No, you can talk to the both of us."

Rooster grimaced. This was the part of the job he hated. The part where he had to do notification, even if the person he was notifying probably wouldn't give a shit what he had to say. He watched as Christine walked over towards the door, pulling the shirt that she wore down past her thighs. "I'm sorry to have to do this, but it has to be by the book."

She nodded.

"You are Christine Herrington, the wife of Clinton Herrington?"

"I am," she nodded. "But I go by Christine Stone now."

"Earlier today a search warrant and arrest warrant was served on Mr. Herrington for the property that housed his home and horse barn. When federal agents tried to execute said search warrant, Mr. Herrington fired on them before turning the gun on himself. He was pronounced dead at the scene from a self-inflicted gunshot wound."

She was in shock. That was the only thing she could think of, because what Rooster was telling her was not computing in her brain. "He killed himself?"

"Yes, in front of no less than twenty agents who were all trying to talk him down."

A little piece of her had known this was how it would end. He wouldn't go to prison, he wouldn't pay for any of his sins here on earth, he had always thought himself better than that. It had always struck her as weird that he thought that way, because out of anyone she knew, including her parents, he had committed the worst.

"There was paperwork found at the scene that you're probably gonna need to take a look at. He had money, it will all come to you," Rooster was saying. "There was also a journal that is really freaky. You might want to read it, you might not. It talks about why he did what he did."

She nodded, not understanding any of it. The only thought that kept rolling through her head was she was free. She was right and truly free. No one would come looking for her again; she didn't have to look over her shoulder. She could go back to her job at the hair salon, live her life with Travis (wherever that took them and whatever it was), and she would be free. "I'm free," she grinned.

"You are," Rooster told her, understanding exactly

what she meant.

The tears came quickly, and she wasn't even sure why. It should have been a relief, and in all reality it was, but the feelings were so intense that she had to release them somehow. "I'm happy about this, is that bad?" she choked out, looking at the two cousins that stood over her.

"No." Rooster shook his head before Travis could answer. "There are bad people in this world, and I'm learning that not everything is clear cut. He was a bad man. This world is going to be better without him. Anyway," he took a step back, "I had to notify you, and now I've done that. I hope this gives you some peace."

"It does, you have no idea how much."

He did have some sort of idea, because he was beginning to feel peace too. The decision he'd made was going to be easier to follow through than he'd ever thought possible. "Well, I'll be seein' y'all."

Travis stopped him, putting his hand on Rooster's arm. "Thanks for coming to tell us."

Rooster motioned Travis out of the room and shut the door. "I'm giving you a heads-up. That was my last official duty. I'm on my way right now to turn in my resignation."

"What?" Travis' mouth opened in shock. "This is what you've wanted to do your entire life…are you kidding me?"

"What I wanted to do was make a fucking difference. Now, after working this job for as long as I have, I find out that my boss and other superiors were just turning their backs as women lay dying? You know as well as I do that they knew about this. They had to. As soon as they start checking financials, I can almost guarantee you there are going to be numerous checks from Clinton Herrington to every single one of them. This isn't who I want to be anymore."

"Who do you want to be?" Travis asked. For the first time in their lives, he was scared for his cousin.

"I don't know, but I know this badge on my chest doesn't make one goddamn bit of difference—to anyone."

The words that would make Rooster feel better never came. There was absolutely nothing that Travis could say that would take away the bitter taste in his cousin's mouth. Nothing. He had based his entire adult life on what was now a lie. He needed some time. "Look, I don't know what to do, what to say, that's going to make you feel better. Having said that, I am here for you. If you need me, it doesn't matter if it's day or night, I will be there."

Rooster knew that, and for the first time in a long time, he believed it. "I know, and I appreciate it more than you know. It's going to take some getting used to."

The two of them didn't say anything else as Rooster turned and made his way towards the front door of the clubhouse. He strode over to the patrol car, got into it, and put it in gear. As he made his way down Porter Pike and back towards town, he remembered the time he'd pulled Liam over. Had it been that long ago? In the grand scheme of things, it hadn't, but to him, it felt like a million years ago.

"Rooster, how ya doin'?" he asked, grinning up at the redheaded sheriff's deputy.

"Not too bad," he answered. It didn't escape Liam's notice that he casually rested his hand on the butt of his gun.

"By the way you're standin' I'll take it this ain't a social call."

"You would be correct in that assumption, and don't be callin'

me Rooster. You of all people know my name is Officer Hancock. We had some reports of loud motorcycles and shots fired out near the old Garvin Lane Bridge. You know anything about that?"

"Can't say that I do. Can you place me or my boys there?"

Officer Hancock smirked. "C'mon Walker, we're old friends."

"That's right, Rooster, we are. We ran these roads when we were teenagers, but we're not on the same side now are we?"

Funny how right when he thought he had his life figured out, it had started changing and now would be the biggest change of all. When he pulled into the parking lot that housed the sheriff cars, he pulled all his equipment and the envelope that held his resignation out of the glove box. The rest of what he took inside was the gear they'd given him. He walked into that building, and within fifteen minutes, he was out. This time he was in plain clothes, and he felt exactly the way Christine had said she had felt. Completely and totally free.

Chapter Twenty-Four

I t felt good being back in his cave. Travis took a deep breath, focusing on all of his video cameras. This was where he felt at peace, where he hadn't felt like he'd been able to come for so long. It was a bad place to be in, not being comfortable in the one place that you felt like you needed to be. He was doing a clean sweep of everything when he heard someone knock on the doorframe. Glancing up, he saw Jagger there. Shit.

"Can I come in?"

"If you promise you ain't gonna bust my head wide open again. I'm finally getting over the motherfuckin' headaches."

Jagger had a seat and stretched his legs out in front of him. "I really wish I could say I was sorry that I did that to you, but I'm not. In fact, I'm still kinda pissed that you kept that from me. I missed all that time with her."

"It wouldn't have been good time, Jagger. Trust me when I tell you this. When I first met her, she was not who she is today. She was closed off from everyone and everything. You think this woman is different from the sister you knew as a child? The woman I met months ago was yet another completely different person. She had to heal a little before she came back to you. Am I sorry that I kept it from you? No. Just like you aren't sorry that you busted my head open. Things happen and we all deal with it."

"I kinda get it, okay? When you're with a woman that you love—and I hope like fuck that you love my sister, because she has had precious little of it in her life—you do what you have to in order to prove that. I also have to admit that part of that disconnect with her was my fault. I should never have left her there. I knew what I was leavin' her with, and that's my own guilt, but I pushed the guilt off on you, and I shouldn't have done that."

The two of them sat in silence for a while. "I wanted to tell you so many times. I even mentioned it to her a few times, but she would shoot me down. I think she was punishing you for leaving her."

"I think so too," Jagger said with a sad smile. "Like I said, though, it's nothing I don't or didn't deserve. I'm just hoping that we can get our relationship back on track. I'm not asking for it to be the same as it was. We've both been to hell and back since the last time we saw each other, but I'm hoping we can come to some semblance of what it was."

Travis' eyes scanned his bank of monitors again, his eyes stopping on one in particular. "I think if anyone can help, it's the woman that Christine's talking to right now."

"I wish we could hear what they were saying," Jagger said, his eyes glued to the monitor.

Christine sat at the hostess counter, glad for some normalcy. Everything that had happened the last few months, especially the last few weeks, had taken its toll on her. Some people wouldn't think a simple receptionist job at a hair salon would mean a lot, but it did to her. It represented everything that had come to mean so much to her. Travis had gotten her this job, she had learned to stand on her own two feet because of this job, and it allowed her to be somewhat of a people person. She looked up as the bell rang, indicating that someone was coming inside. Her breath caught when she saw it was B.

"Hey," B waved, her smile was bright, her body language open.

She could tell why her brother loved the other woman. She was gorgeous, and seemed to be very sweet. Christine very badly wanted to get to know her, but she knew that would come in time. They couldn't automatically be the best of friends just because she'd come back into their lives. "Hey, you have an appointment with Shelby, right?" She went about checking the appointment calendar for the day.

"I do," B nodded, but it's not for a few hours. "I was actually wondering if you'd like to go have coffee with me." She pointed to the coffee house across the square. "I know this is your job, but if we tried to talk at the clubhouse, there are two men who would be very interested in what we had to say to one another. And if Travis is anything like Jagger, he knows what time you're supposed to be home." She rolled her eyes, an indulgent smile on her face.

"Go on," Shelby said from the main floor. "We'll be fine for a while. You hardly ever take a break as it is."

She grabbed her purse and followed B out the door.

"It's a gorgeous day," Bianca said as the two of them made their way across the square. "Can you believe it's going to be Thanksgiving in a few weeks?"

"No." She shook her head. "I didn't even realize that."

"As a teacher, you tend to have every available day off on a countdown on your phone." Bianca flashed a smile at her.

"I could understand that! I'm sure it's a very rewarding yet trying profession."

"It is. I love it! I wouldn't give it up for anything—even though I've only been doing it since August."

They arrived at the coffee house and went inside. There wasn't a line, so they placed their orders and waited for them to be filled. Once they had the mugs in their hands, Bianca directed them towards the back so that they could have some privacy. Christine had never been inside this place, but she immediately loved the feel of it, the exposed brick wall, the smell of coffee and food. They had a seat, and for a few moments, there was an awkward silence until Bianca opened her mouth again and began to speak.

"I want you to know that Jagger is the most important part of my life. Teaching is what I love to do, I wouldn't want another profession, but Jagger is the best thing that has ever happened to me. He's made me feel things and experience things that I never thought I would ever be able to. Like most of the people that stay at the clubhouse, life hasn't always been easy for me." She stopped to take a drink of her coffee, and it seemed to pull her together. "I know that the two of you aren't really talking right now, and I know that's killing him. I'm not asking you to divulge secrets to me, because that's your personal business, but I want to be more forthcoming with you than I'm sure he's been."

Christine wasn't sure if she was supposed to say anything, but she really did want to understand Jagger better. They had both changed in the years since they had seen each other. They had grown up and moved on and had a million things happen to them. She didn't want to be estranged from him, so if the way to understand what he was going through was going to be through Bianca, then she was okay with that.

"He tried to find you, he did. I know he did. There have been times this year that I've seen him talk to people who may have known where you were, but it was such a secret. He couldn't find your parents. Now that we know they were among the mass grave, we know why. He had nothing to go on." She wanted to reiterate that to Christine, maybe if they kept telling her how badly Jagger had tried to right things, she would finally believe them.

Finding out her parents had been two of the bodies in the graves had not really been a surprise to Christine, but she had still felt the loss. No matter how bad her home life had been, those were still the people who had given her life. If she was honest, she was having a hard time coping with it all. The nightmares were back, and she'd not had them for months before this reoccurrence. "I know. I know with everything that I am he tried to find me. To be honest, the person holding back is me." She put her hand on her chest.

"Can you tell me why? He would love nothing more than for you to come to him and tell him what you need."

"I would love that too." She smiled sadly. "There's so

much finally going right in my world, but I just can't seem to reconcile that with who I am today." Tears flooded her eyes. They had been doing that a lot lately, more than they ever had in her life. It hadn't been horrible until she'd seen the front page of the newspaper. That paper talked about just how many bodies were in that field, how long it had been going on—much longer than she had been at that house, but she felt so much guilt. How and why had she been the only one to survive when so many hadn't?

"Are you feeling guilty?" Bianca asked. She recognized that look in Christine's eyes. It was one she had carried for a while after she had been taken hostage. It wasn't that she felt guilty that something had happened to Raymond Tucker and she had lived, but she felt guilty for even causing the events in the first place. If he hadn't become obsessed with her, there would have been no reason for him to stalk her, take her hostage, and put all those children in harm's way.

Christine squeezed her eyes shut and nodded. "I am." It felt good to admit that; she hadn't been able to admit it to even Travis. She knew that he would question why when she should be feeling so blessed that she had fought and made it out alive. When Christine opened her eyes again, Bianca held a card out to her.

"This woman is absolutely amazing. I've gone to her, your brother has gone to her, Layne has gone to her, Meredith and Tyler have gone to her. She'll get you fixed right up."

She grabbed the card out of Bianca's hand and read the words, remembering that Meredith had also mentioned someone to her. "This is a psych doctor?" she hated the implications of that.

"Oh honey, she's so much more. She's your cheerleader, the mother or grandmother you never had, she doesn't judge you, but she doesn't coddle you either. Doc Jones will shoot it to you straight, and you'll wonder why you didn't go before. She has made a huge difference in a lot of people's lives."

Christine flipped the card over and over in her hand.

Bianca took a drink from her coffee. "I'm just going to tell you straight. I pray with everything I have that I'm your sister-in-law one day—soon, hopefully—if your brother could take a motherfuckin' hint."

That caused a smile to tilt the side of Christine's lips.

"I can see how badly you're hurting, and I don't want that for anyone, much less someone who's going to be my family. Please, accept this and the help that I know she can give you. It's not weakness to admit you need help, no matter what your parents told you. It's the bravest thing in the world you can do."

At those words, Christine completely lost it, sobbing quietly. "You get it?"

"I do." Bianca grabbed her hand. "I do, and you will get no judgment from me. If you want me to take you there, I will. I will do whatever I can to help repair the relationship between you and Jagger. You mean so much to him."

"I want to repair it too, and I want my relationship with Travis to be strong."

"It's going to take time," Bianca warned her. "For people like us that have grown up not believing that we have any bit of good in us, it takes time."

"I'm willing to put the work in. I don't want to be this meek woman anymore."

"Then you won't be."

That was all Christine needed to hear, it was like a light switched on inside her. Someone that hadn't known her believed in her, and that felt good. It felt like she really could be different and that gave her hope.

Chapter Twenty-Five

C hristine rubbed her hands against the denim of her jeans and took a deep breath.

"You sure you want to do this?" Jagger asked. He stood behind her, Steele at her side, Bianca at his.

"If you do, I do. I think we need to. This is the one thing that's been holding me back; I need to make peace with it."

She felt Jagger's hand on her shoulder as she ascended the old porch steps. It had been a long two months of counseling that she'd undergone. Sometimes Travis would come and sit in with her, sometimes Jagger would. Every time, she and Doc Jones would work on some part of her childhood or adulthood that had caused her anxiety. At her last session, Jagger had been there, and Doc Jones suggested that the two of them go back to their childhood home, together. She thought that it would go a long way in making them feel better about the way things had gone down. It would give them a sense of closure that neither one of them ever had.

"I do," he told her.

"If you two don't mind," she addressed Travis and Bianca, "I think Jagger and I need to go in by ourselves for a few minutes, just to get over the initial shock."

"Whatever you want," Bianca was quick to assure her. "It's a little creepy out here, but as long as Travis is here to chase the boogeyman away, I'll be fine." She reached over, grabbing Travis' arm for effect.

Jagger chuckled, glad for her humor. They were going to need it.

Travis reached down, kissing Christine quickly. "She's right; we'll be out here if you two need anything. Probably her protecting me, she's got that smart-ass mouth on her," he grinned, hoping for some lightheartedness before the two of them went into the house.

Christine grinned back before taking a deep breath and grabbing Jagger's hand. They were going to do this together. "You ready?" she asked him.

His breath was heavy in his chest. He'd hated this house so much as a kid and then a teenager. It had been such an unhappy home. He hated to even be this close to it now, but he knew that she was right—if they didn't get over this, they were never going to be able to move on with their lives. That was the one thing they both desperately needed. They both had people that loved them in ways they had never been loved before. It was time to put the past where it was supposed to be, in the past.

"As I'll ever be."

When they reached the front door and turned the knob, both of them were surprised to find that it was locked, after all this time.

"You wanna do a little B&E?"

She couldn't help the giggle that escaped her mouth. It broke the tension, and for that she was extremely grateful.

"I've never done that before."

"Travis, we need to do a little B&E," he called over his shoulder.

Travis walked up the front porch steps, casually putting his arm around Christine's shoulders. "You wanna learn how to do it, or do you want me to get us in?"

There was something about being there with him and him teaching her how to be the kind of rule-breaker that he was that made her feel like a badass. Didn't necessarily mean that she wanted to do it, but it felt good to be asked. She bit her lip and shook her head. "Nah, you go ahead."

"If you say so."

She watched as Jagger moved back to give him room to work. Travis pulled a toolkit out of his pocket and bent down to inspect the lock.

"Why don't y'all just bust the door in?" Bianca asked from where she stood, her eyes covered with sunglasses to protect them from the strong winter sun.

"Shush and let the man work," Jagger quieted her. "I happen to like watchin' Steele pick a lock. It's pretty damn cool."

In less than a minute's time, he had the door open. "Got it."

Christine waited until Bianca and Jagger went in, and then put her arms around Travis' neck. "That was hot."

"Picking a lock?" he asked, his eyebrows raised in question.

"Something about the way you were focused on that lock. I only see that level of focus with you when we're alone."

And just like that, he was surprised by her. He found

himself being surprised by her more and more lately. Since Clinton had died, more and more of her personality was coming out. He loved that and hoped that it wouldn't stop. "Let's hurry up and get this over with, then we can go be alone again."

She grinned at him, thankful that he was as playful as she was. She knew that it had taken her a while to get comfortable with things, and she wasn't completely sure she would ever be over some of the things that had happened to her, but she loved him, and she loved that he was in her life. She didn't say it enough, but she hoped that he knew just how much he meant to her. She hadn't ever loved anyone besides her brother, and she was learning to give that feeling to someone else. It was difficult, but she was trying. "You're right, the quicker we get through this, the quicker we can put it behind us."

Jagger held out his hand, clasping hers tightly. They had lived in this home together and he needed her support to walk over this threshold and back into a life they had both left. They didn't make it much further than the front room.

He felt like he was stuck in a time warp. Save for the dust, nothing had changed since he had left at eighteen. He could still feel the emotions he had when he stepped into the house from a long day at school—the fear and anxiousness.

"It hasn't changed at all," he breathed.

"No, they didn't change anything when you left; they even kept your room the same. They wouldn't let anyone in there. We sometimes had guests—you know, members of the church—they were never allowed to sleep in your room," Christine told him.

They made their way into the kitchen and dining room area. "This is the one part of the house I absolutely hated," she told the rest of them. "This is where we would get our sermons from him, as we ate dinner, because he knew that he would have our attention. There wasn't a way to escape."

"Then, if you didn't agree with the wisdom that he imparted on you at dinner, he would take you out back to the woodshed afterwards. It all began and ended here," Jagger added.

"That didn't change after you left either. Those two were so set in their ways. It's weird because the two of them were meant for each other. They obviously shared a very deep connection to let him do what he did for so long, and I never got the feeling that Mom was scared of him."

"Me neither," Jagger agreed. "She always defaulted to what he wanted her to do. I hated that. I wanted her to stand on her own two feet."

"Well, you never have to worry about that with me, babe," Bianca rubbed her hand up and down his back.

The rest of them laughed. Bianca made it a point usually to never listen to what Jagger told her, even though what he wanted was for her own good.

They went through the house, attempting to go into every room. Christine hated the feeling the house gave her, it was like it was suffocating her. She felt the same kind of brick on her chest that she had felt when she lived there. "I hate this house," she said when they made it through the downstairs. "I hate everything this house represents."

"Me too," Jagger agreed. "But I feel like we need to see this through. We're never going to move on, if we don't."

She nodded, knowing that he was right, but it didn't make it any easier. They made it through the rest of the house, both stopping at their bedrooms one last time. Jagger walked into his room and took a look around. "Y'all wanna see a secret?"

They were all intrigued, so they all agreed.

He strode over to where a picture of the Ten Commandments rested against the wallpaper and pulled it back from the wall. Underneath it sat a poster of a Harley. "It was my own little rebellion," he explained, laughing.

"Oh my God," Christine giggled. "I can't believe I never knew it was there."

"I was very careful. You know what he would have done to me if he knew I defiled his Godly home with that, but I had to do something. This place was so stuffy and stodgy. I had to have something that was mine and only mine. It was the only thing I could think of at the time."

Travis leaned with his back against the wall. "What finally made you decide to leave?"

Jagger had a seat on the bed. "It was the day of my eighteenth birthday and I had gone to a tattoo parlor. I got this." He pointed to his forearm, where he had a saying of some sort. It was now buried beneath the other tats he had, and it wasn't so easy to read anymore. "My dad took one look at it and told me the devil had gotten to me. I wouldn't be able to stay in his house until I let him beat it out of me. He wanted to take me back to the woodshed again."

Christine shivered. She hated that damn woodshed. She hadn't been taken there near as often as Jagger, but the few times she had were ingrained in her memory.

"We got there, and I reminded him that me being eighteen, I could now fight back, and if he dared use his belt on me, he better be prepared for me to use it on him. I wasn't as big as I am now, but I had been lifting a little back then. I was still bigger than him, but he thought I was lying or joking, I'm not sure which. He came after me with it, and I grabbed it in my hand and turned it on him. I beat the shit out of him. He threatened to call the police on me, and I told him to go ahead, that I wasn't scared of him anymore. I wore scars, I still wear scars, and I knew Christine had them too. I told him we'd put his ass in jail and he would never get out. I guess it scared him enough that he actually believed me. He told me to get out and never look back. I asked if I could go get my stuff, and he told me no…if I was an adult, I'd figure it out."

"Damn, dude," Travis said from where he stood. Christine had come to stand in front of him, and he slipped his arms around her waist, resting his chin against her shoulder. He'd had times in his childhood and early adulthood that had been rough. His mom had never been able to understand that his brain worked fast and he didn't have the aptitude to do the things she wanted him to, but she hadn't ever told him to get out of her house. That had been his decision.

"Yeah, so I left. It was the best and worst decision of my life. Best for me, probably worst for Christine. I'm sorry about that." He looked up at her. "But I couldn't stay here anymore."

"I know," she told him. "And regardless of what you think, I've never blamed you for it. You're my brother and I love you. I love the man you've become and the people that you've brought into my life. This place," she gestured at the house, "it doesn't define us anymore. Let's get the fuck outta here."

That was one thing they could all agree on, and without one backwards glance, they walked out and away from it. This time, for good.

Chapter Twenty-Six

Christine lay that night in Travis' arms, her head resting against his chest, listening to his heart beat strongly. This had quickly become her favorite place in the world. She loved that he would take off his shirt, open his arms, and expect her to snuggle up next to him. That heartbeat was what got her through the hard days, and the smile that he gave her was what made the other ones so easy. He had been there through everything, and she knew that she gotten lucky. She hadn't ever known another man who had loved her as unconditionally as he did. He might not have said the words, but he proved it to her every day in everything thing he did.

"Are you okay?" he asked, running his hands up and down her back. "I know that couldn't have been easy for you."

When they had gotten back to the clubhouse, Liam had called a meeting and set run schedules for the next few weeks, and he hadn't had a chance to talk to her. Things were getting back to normal now, and he wanted to make sure that she wasn't being looked over in the busyness of everything else.

"It wasn't easy, but honestly, it was easier than I

thought it would be. It gave me anxiety, just like I knew that it would, but it didn't define me. It didn't break me. There was a point in my life that it would have. I'm in a good place now though, because of you and the people that you've brought into my life, but mostly because of you."

He turned them so that he could look into her eyes. "I wish I had known you back then."

"No you don't," she laughed. "I was a much different person, and I was still scared of everything. I wouldn't have been receptive to your advances. Believe it or not, when you met me, I was at the absolutely worst point in my life. My car had broken down, I had no money, I was living in the CRISIS center, I had never been that far down. Even when I lived in Clinton's house, I wasn't that far down because I didn't know what reality was. It was a harsh slap in the face, but then here you came."

"You make me sound like I made a huge sacrifice. I didn't. And let's not forget, your hair was an awful color," he laughed, running his hands through the strands that were now rich and healthy.

She smacked him on the chest, choosing to ignore the hair comment. "You did," she insisted. "You didn't know me from anyone, but there you were, protecting me, helping me find a house to live in, a reliable car, a job, and you never ever asked for anything in return. I always expected you to, but you never did. Do you know how many nights I had lingerie laid out because I figured you would be trying to cash in on what you had done for me?"

Travis grinned. "You really thought I would do something like that?"

"I didn't know you, but I knew you would be different

than Clinton, and I wanted to be prepared, as weird as that sounds. I always wanted to be the type of woman for you that other women could be for other men." That had always been her goal, and she realized now that would always be her goal. She wanted them to have a normal relationship, she wanted them to argue, fight, make up, and enjoy life.

"Trust me, babe, you've never disappointed me."

That felt good. She was glad that she hadn't disappointed him, because she knew there were times when she could have. "I find that hard to believe, but thank you."

"What do you want to do, now that you have all this freedom and money?" he asked, referencing the fact that she was no longer married and Clinton had more money than either of them knew what to do with.

She sighed. "I'm going to use that money for something good. Meredith and I have something up our sleeves, but we don't want to share it with anybody just yet." She winked at him, situating herself closer.

If it gave her something to do and a reason to stay here, stay with his family, then he was all for it. Anything that would keep her around. He was still so scared she would leave, that now she didn't need him. She could stand on her own two feet; he didn't have to be behind her anymore, holding her up.

"Where do you see us going?" he asked, scared to ask her the question but needing to know.

"I don't know," she told him truthfully. "I know that I don't want anyone but you, and I know that there's never been anyone more perfect for me other than you. I see myself growing up with you, changing and evolving, being the person that I want to be. Does that mean we stay together forever? I don't have that answer, and neither do you."

That was a start. As much as he wanted the formal answer right now, he knew that he couldn't ask her to give him that. They had both been through something together that not many people had gone through. He was still learning how to deal with her and what she needed; she was still learning how to live a normal life. "We still have work to do?"

She shook her head. "I still have work to do. All that I ask is that you don't get irritated with me, you let me know that I'm trying your patience, but please don't give up on me."

He scooted closer to her, putting his hands on her face and bringing her close to him. "I've never once thought of giving up on you. You've gotta know that by now. I either love the fuck outta you or I'm a glutton for punishment."

A slow smile spread across her face, and she threw herself at him, burying her head in his shoulder. This right here was where she felt safest, and she knew that she never wanted to let this go. "I love you too," she whispered. "I didn't know what that meant before I met you, but you show me every day what that means. Your faith in me is what's gotten me through."

"No." He pushed her hair back from her face, licking his dry lips. It had done something crazy to his heart when she said she loved him back. "Your faith in *me* has gotten me through. You've always trusted me and I've never deserved it. Together, we're going to make a life for ourselves; we're going to carve out our own niche and make our own family. I promise you that."

A family of her own, one that she could love, one that she could be free with. Those words were the most beautiful that she had ever heard.

Epilogue

Travis Steele sat in front of his bank of monitors, doing what he did best. After the past few months, he had to admit that besides with Christine, this was where he felt the absolute most comfortable. Grabbing a sucker, he opened it and stuck the piece of candy in his mouth, rolling it around with his tongue. Rolling his neck on his shoulders, he readjusted his glasses and took note of the time. It was getting to be late evening, and Christine should be getting home.

"Hey, babe." She appeared in the doorframe.

"I was just thinking that you should be getting home anytime now," he told her, moving back from the desk so that she could come sit in his lap.

"B and I got our hair highlighted at the shop," she explained, having a seat where he patted his thigh. She reached over, taking his glasses off and sitting them on the desk.

He took the invitation and buried his face in her hair. He loved the smell of it after she got it done. There was something about the products they used at the salon. He loved it.

"You like?" she asked, a sly smirk on her face.

"I love," he answered, leaning against the cushioned back of the chair.

She looked at him, her eyebrows coming together.

"What?" he asked, laughing when she ran her hands over the hair that had begun to grow back on top of his head. He'd been worried that it might not grow back; it was taking a long time.

"I've always had this question about you, but I've never asked it."

He cupped her thigh with his hand, slightly stroking it. "The answer is no, I've never had sex in here, but I would love to break in this chair."

She threw her head back, laughing loudly. "You perv, that's not at all what I wanted to ask you!"

The smile on her face was easier coming now, and he liked to think that was partially because of him. He would do anything to bring that smile to her face. "Oh, okay, what is it you wanted to know?"

"These." She picked up his glasses. "Did you lie to me when you told me you didn't really need them? You're wearing them a lot more lately, and I'm wondering if you're trying to be hipster, like Tyler says, or do you really need them?"

He grabbed them from her hands. "Okay, okay, I do need them, but only when I have eye strain, which I do have right now. Can you move to the left just a minute," he asked her, distracted suddenly.

She worried that something was happening, so she didn't even question it. Christine turned so that she could see what he saw. "Isn't that Rooster?" she asked.

"Yeah, and that's Roni's apartment."

They watched as he parked and walked up to the door. He didn't even knock, he had the code. Travis sat there with raised eyebrows. Only Liam had the code to her apartment. She was very careful with who she gave it to. Both he and Christine glanced at each other, the surprise evident on their faces, and then they laughed at what they had just seen.

"Wow," he breathed. He, like all of them, had known they'd had a relationship as teenagers, but he didn't know they were still hanging out with each other now. Travis looked at Christine, a grin on his face. "Guess we're not the only two that have had a dirty little secret."

The End

Heaven Hill #6

(Coming Late Fall 2014)

Prologue

Sharon—better known as Roni—Walker, sighed deeply. Today was her thirty-fifth birthday, and just what the fuck did she have to show for it? Not a damn thing. She had spent most of her life bowing down to a father who didn't care one iota about her and living for a brother that she had found out wasn't exactly her brother. Half-brother, but not full-blood. Funny, that fact seemed to bother her more than it did Liam; it had taken a part of her life away that she hadn't realized she counted on. Her life had been taking care of Liam since their mother had left. Now it almost felt like she'd done it for no good reason.

Her phone went off from where it sat beside her. More happy birthday messages, these from her niece and nephew, Mandy and Drew. She loved those kids with everything she had, and she would absolutely do anything that they asked her to, but today, they made her sad. Her best years had been spent on people who didn't give a shit about her, and now here she was—thirty-five and bitter.

This time, a knock sounded at her door. She contemplated not opening it, not even going to check and see who it was. She wanted to wallow in her own self-pity and be miserable. It was her birthday, and damnit, she was allowed to do that if she wanted to. Checking the peephole, she saw the one person that she wanted to see, so she knew she had to let him in.

"Hey, Rooster," she greeted as she opened the door.

"Hey." He grinned at her, rocking back on his feet. "Happy birthday!"

She tried to keep the smile from her face, but she couldn't help smiling back at him. "Thank you."

"Why aren't you out celebrating? I figured there'd be a big shindig at the clubhouse."

"They wanted one," she told him as she ushered him inside her apartment. "But I'm not feelin' it this year. I'm an old bitter Betty."

"Let's get outta here." He jerked his head in the direction of the parking lot.

"Where are we gonna go?"

"I don't know," he pulled her to the window and opened the blinds, showing her the bike he'd ridden over. "But I got my bike out, and it still runs. Take a ride with me."

That had been her favorite thing to do that summer— the one before everything changed. For just a few minutes, she wanted to relive that feeling, relive that place that she had never been able to get back to.

"It's cold still. You know that, right?"

"Early March is usually cold, I got it covered."

She didn't want to know how he had it covered, but she desperately wanted to take this ride with him, so she grabbed her jacket and boots. Without a look back at the DVR she had been planning to catch up on, she followed him out the door. It looked like wallowing and self-pity were going to have to take a backseat—at least for this night.

Acknowledgements

Allison, for always being there with me through all of this. I don't think it would be the same experience if you weren't here with me. One day, we'll see our names in bright lights! :)

My friends and family, thank you for being as understanding as possible when it comes to my writing. I know sometimes you all wonder why I'm spending so much time doing it, but it is something that I truly love, and it's brought a lot to all of our lives. I appreciate you all not giving me too much shit about it!

Slick, Didi, Halos & Horns, Swept Away by Romance, Mariann's Book Blog, and the other blogs and Facebook Pages that have taken a chance on me and the series. I can't thank you enough!

There are a whole bunch of people that make Heaven Hill happen and keep me on task. Thank you so much for everything that you do and all the support that you give! This isn't always easy, but you all make it worthwhile!

Connect with Laramie

Website:
http://www.laramiebriscoe.com

Facebook:
https://www.facebook.com/AuthorLaramieBriscoe

Twitter:
https://twitter.com/LaramieBriscoe

Pinterest:
http://www.pinterest.com/laramiebriscoe/

Instagram:
http://instagram.com/laramie_briscoe

Substance B:
http://substance-b.com/LaramieBriscoe.html

Email:
Laramie.briscoe@gmail.com

Also by Laramie Briscoe

Only the Beginning
Rockin' Country #1

Chapter One

The crowd screamed loudly, causing her palms to sweat and her heart to race. Harmony Stewart inhaled deeply and then exhaled, letting the breath flow through her. The relaxation technique worked. Shoulders that had been so tight she couldn't even roll them were now loose. It was always like this, she realized. Right before she went on stage, the nervous energy started, causing her to tense up—not fully being able to appreciate the life she was living. Closing her eyes, she breathed again, feeling her muscles loosen up even more.

"Harmony, you're up next."

She nodded, glancing at the production tech. "Thanks." Her voice was thin even to her own ears. This was just something that she went through, no matter how many millions of albums she sold or awards she garnered.

Looking out onto the stage, she saw the rock group, Black Friday, finishing up. A fan of the band, she tried to still the heart that threatened to beat out of her chest as they finished their song and walked towards her. The lead singer was the personification of hotness in her opinion. She had always wanted a meeting, but had never been able to approach him when they had been in the same space. This time he would have to walk right by her—not that she had deluded herself to think he would know who she even was. Pulling her shaking hands to her body, she gripped them hard as the group approached.

"Good job, guys," she smiled as they passed her. One by one, they nodded and accepted her smile until she came face to face with Reaper, the lead singer. She only knew his stage name. What she wouldn't give to know his real one.

"Thanks. Good luck out there, sweetheart," he smiled widely. His teeth were white and straight, the dimples that she had caught glimpses of in pictures deepened widely in his cheeks. He was tall, much taller than she had originally thought. He towered over her 5'6 frame (with heels, thank you very much), and the tattoos that traveled down his arms were a feast to her eyes. They were intricate, and she wished she had the time to study them all.

Harmony opened her mouth to tell him something else, but he was already gone. Disappointment hit her stomach hard and fast. But at least it had been a start. With any luck, she would see him at some other award show. She heard her cue as she looked back to where the rock band stood, debriefing with some of their management. For just a split second, her eyes met Reaper's and goose bumps appeared on her arms. If only they'd had more time.

Reaper sat with his head back, eyes closed. The night had been long. He never really liked doing these awards shows, but their fans were amazing. Even though they didn't have what others called "crossover" success, they had some of the most rabid fans in the music industry. That, however, didn't change the fact that he was lonely and tired of not having someone besides the members of his band to share his life with.

"Who was the cutie that smiled at us as we walked by?"

"That was Harmony Stewart," he answered, moving only his lips.

"Country singer?"

"Yes, dude," he sighed. "The country singer."

"She's cuter than I imagined. I've only seen her on TV a few times."

Reaper sighed again. "Seriously Train, you're getting on my fuckin' nerves. Do you have to talk all the time?"

"What's your problem? Do you need to get laid?" Train asked, having a seat next to his friend.

"Do you ever get sick of all this?" He lifted his long arms and big hands up; gesturing to the backstage green room they sat in.

"Sick of what? The free pussy, the free booze, the amazing trips overseas and around this great nation? Playing the music we love every night? I'm ready to do this the rest of my life. Why aren't you?"

Reaper lifted his head up and opened his eyes, staring into the eyes of his friend. "I'm burnt out. Not with the music, but with the lifestyle. I need a change, something different to shake things up."

"Burnt out? How can you be burnt out?"

"It's just…" he ran his fingers through his hair. "We've been on the road for a year. I need something new and exciting in my life. I'm sick of the same girls, the same bus, and the same hotel rooms."

"You're bein' a moody fucking pansy is what you're being. Do you know how many guys would give their left nut to be where we are?" Train slapped his friend on the shoulder, the disbelief showing on his face.

Reaper realized he would get nowhere with his friend. Train dealt with his demons in unhealthy ways and perhaps tonight wasn't the best time to approach him about this. He couldn't rightfully explain his feelings if he didn't fully understand them himself. Better to just pretend that everything was peachy. "You're right. I'm crazy. I just need some good alcohol and a good cigarette. Let's get to the after party."

"Now that's what I'm talkin' about," the lead guitarist said, grabbing his friend by the arm and ushering him out of the room.

Reaper realized that nobody seemed to care what he thought, how he felt, or just how lonely he was. He might as well make the best of what to him was an unbearable situation.

"Harmony? Are you changing into the dress that new designer sent you for the after party?"

"I think so," Harmony answered her best friend and assistant, Shell.

"You need to change now, then."

Harmony rolled her eyes and grabbed the hanger from Shell's hand. "Yes ma'am."

Used to bossing her friend around, Shell had a seat while Harmony changed. "So tell me, did you meet anybody interesting at this awards show?"

"I did. Did you see any of the show?"

"I didn't get a chance too, no. I wish I had, but there was a lot going on back here," Shell answered from behind the door that Harmony had closed to change.

"I'm so sorry, Shell. I know how hard you work, and you'll never fully know how much I appreciate it. You'll be excited to hear that I finally met the guys from Black Friday."

Harmony heard the squeal and couldn't help the smile that spread across her face.

"I am so damn jealous. That lead singer—was he as hot as he looks on TV?"

"Even more so. I actually said a few words to him. Top moment of my life this year—for real."

She finished changing and let herself out of the dressing room. Coming out, she turned around in a circle, making sure everything looked okay. For the show, Harmony had wanted to keep it classy and her dress had been very Old Hollywood. This dress, however, was young and fun. Sparkles and glitter reigned. The hot pink color showed off the tan she had been able to get during a short vacation before awards season ramped up.

"Does this look okay?" she asked, turning around again so Shell could see her from every angle.

"You look really good. Hoping to meet anybody at this party?"

"You never know," she shrugged. "Maybe the guys from Black Friday will be there, and I'll be able to say something else to them. I was kind of a blabbering fool earlier. Are you coming with me?"

Shell wrinkled her nose up at her friend. "I don't know. This hasn't been a stellar day for me."

"All the more reason for you to raid my closet, find something hot, and come out on the town with me."

"Why are you trying to corrupt me? Usually it's the other way around. You're the belle of the country ball, and I'm the one trying to get you to do Jager shots," Shell laughed.

"Maybe I'm ready to let my hair down. It's time. I am twenty-four years old, and I'm not gettin' any younger. If I keep goin' at this pace with the music, I'm not goin' to be married before thirty, and that's never who I wanted to be. I'm the type of girl who wants a boyfriend, wants to be in love. I'm gonna have to make that a priority."

Shell knew that Harmony was telling the truth. She was one of those women who were made to be in love, but she wasn't for sure that her friend had ever felt those feelings. Her one serious relationship hadn't ended well and left her feeling disconnected. It was nice to see that she was beginning to look past that time in her life. "Okay, okay. If I need to be there to keep you from asking the first man you meet to marry you, I'll be there to save you from yourself."

"You, Shell, are the best friend a girl could ask for." She reached over, kissing her on the cheek.

"You sure we can leave in an hour?" Reaper asked he unfolded himself from the backseat of the limo they had taken to the party location.

"Yes, I'm sure," Train answered with a huff. Reaper didn't miss the way he wiped the back of his hand over his nose. It was a sure sign that some things never changed. He raised his eyebrows as Train admonished him. "Dude, when did you become such a fucking killjoy?"

"I told you already, I'm just not feeling this tonight."

They got into line with the rest of the celebrities and the other members of their band to walk the red carpet that lead into the venue that housed the party for the night.

"Hey." Train hit his friend's elbow. "Isn't that the little country girl from earlier?" He pointed further up the carpet.

Reaper couldn't see for shit, so he squinted his eyes together, trying to bring the person in front of them better in focus. "Fuck," he mumbled, pulling the wrap-around sunglasses he normally wore on stage up to his eyes. They were part of his persona, but in actuality they were prescription and without them—he really couldn't see. "Yeah, that's her."

"Cute, isn't she?"

"Seriously man, we already talked about how cute she is."

At that moment, they walked onto the main part of the carpet. Flashbulbs went off as they plastered smiles on their faces. Photographers called their names from all around. A little further down the aisle a photographer yelled at Reaper.

"What sweetheart? Didn't hear you." He cupped his hand over his ear.

"Take a picture with Harmony. It'll be a good photo op."

Harmony heard the exchange from where she stood and laughed. "He might not want to be seen with someone like me," she smiled as she glanced back at him.

He couldn't tell if she was flirting with him or not, but he figured he would seize the day. "Nah, darlin' maybe you don't wanna be seen with someone like me."

A blush covered her face, and she turned around so that she faced him. "I'm a fan, seriously. I'd love to take a picture with you."

The smile she gave him made his stomach dance. He had faced huge crowds before overseas. Hundreds of thousands of people he had performed in front of and not been nervous. Approaching this woman with the smile on her face made his legs shake. He strode over to her and easily put his arm around her waist. Even wearing heels she only came up to his shoulder.

"Where do you want us to look?" he asked.

The amount of people screaming at them was so deafening neither one of them could understand what anyone was saying. "Let's just start looking to the left and then look to the right," she said as she gripped his waist.

They stood there for long minutes as everyone got their pictures—and when it was over, the two of them were reluctant to let go of each other.

"Thanks Reaper and Harmony," the original photographer told them.

"You're welcome," Harmony answered. She pulled her arm from around his waist and turned to face him. "Thanks for taking a picture with me. I guess I'll see you inside and maybe, just maybe, I'll learn what people call you besides Reaper?"

"If I tell you that, then I'd have to kill you. It's highly classified." He put his hands in the pockets of the pants he wore and rocked back on his heels.

She wasn't sure if he was flirting with her or not because she couldn't see his eyes, but she knew that they were staring right at her. "Well then, I guess I better figure out how to work on my security clearance." She gave him a flip of her hair as she turned from him and walked towards the entrance of the club.

The pictures were already making their way all over the world.

The Heaven Hill Series

Meant to Be
(First in the Heaven Hill Series)

Single mother.

Laid off factory worker.

Drug runner for the Heaven Hill Motorcycle Club.

When Denise Cunningham is served with foreclosure papers on her birthday it's the last straw in a long line of bad luck. Sitting and crying about things has never been how she solved her problems, but this time she decides to do just that. A phone call interrupts her pity party and changes the course of her life forever.

Loyal brother.

Grease monkey mechanic.

Vice President of the Heaven Hill Motorcycle Club.

William Walker Jr., known as Liam to his club, needs a new recruit that is just naïve enough and desperate enough to do what he asks without question. When Denise Cunningham lands in his lap, he decides to hire her—not because he wants to, because he has to.

Neither are comfortable in their new roles, but he needs help and she can't stand to lose anything else.

As bullets fly and a local Bowling Green, KY reporter works to bring the club down, Liam and Denise find themselves getting closer to one another. When the stakes get high and outside forces try to keep them away from each other, they have to decide if they really are meant to be.

Out of Darkness
(Second in the Heaven Hill Series)

Ex-News reporter.

Rape survivor.

Former enemy of the Heaven Hill MC.

Meredith Rager's life completely changed the night she was attacked by an unknown person. Once a vibrant force that threatened everything about Heaven Hill, she is now under their care. The only place she feels safe is inside their compound. When she decides to take back the part of her life that her rapist took away, she discovers secrets that once again could tear the club apart.

Orphan.

Formidable force of nature.

Loved member of the Heaven Hill MC.

Tyler Blackfoot came into the world a John Doe. An orphan from the moment that he took his first breath, the only thing anyone knew was his Native American heritage. For most of his life, he's been alone – except for the club that has taken him in as their own. When he rescued Meredith, a protective side of his personality came out that he never knew he had. Protecting her means everything – even when he discovers danger might be closer than either of them thought possible.

Together, the two of them are trying to make a life for themselves. Against everything they have, they're hoping to see the light that will lead them out of darkness.

Losing Control
(Third in the Heaven Hill Series)

Strip-club waitress.
Aspiring teacher.
Friend of the Heaven Hill MC.

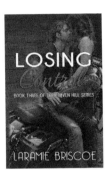

Bianca Hawks met Jagger Stone in the most embarrassing of ways. After watching him play music at Wet Wanda's for months, she fell half naked into his arms after a drunken bout with a stripper pole and the back of a pick-up truck. Avoiding him and his killer smile no longer works when she needs her car repaired and he comes to her rescue. His request for payment comes in the form of date nights spent with just the two of them – away from both the strip club and the MC.

Tough guy with model good looks.
Talented musician.
Newly patched member of the Heaven Hill MC.

Jagger Stone only wanted two things – to be a patched member of the Heaven Hill MC and to get to know Bianca Hawks. One for two isn't bad, but when her car breaks down and she's left with no one else to help her, he plays the situation to his advantage. Over late nights driving up and down the interstate and nights in spent at her apartment, Jagger realizes that there is so much more to Bianca than he ever knew.

When her dream of becoming a school teacher is threatened by someone who wants her all to himself, the two of them are thrown into a dangerous game of cat and mouse. For the first time, Heaven Hill isn't sure what they are up against or if they can keep their family safe. In times of danger, Bianca and Jagger know the only thing they can do is hold onto each other while trying not to admit they are losing control.

Worth the Battle
(Fourth in the Heaven Hill Series)

Movie star running from her life.
Secret writer of erotic romance.
Trusts only Layne O'Connor of the Heaven Hill MC.

When Jessica Shea fears that her privacy is in danger, she takes the drastic step to leave her life behind and escape to the only person who's never treated her like the movie star she is. He's the one person who's never sold a story to the tabloids and who knows the real Jessica, the one underneath the makeup and high-gloss shine of Hollywood.

Their friendship has stood the test of time. Now, someone has stolen private photos and writings from her home. Things that she doesn't want the public at large to see. There's only one place she knows she can go to be under the radar and lick her wounds.

That place is wherever Layne O'Connor is.

War Veteran.
Striving to live a normal life.
Member of the Heaven Hill MC.

Layne left a piece of himself in the war zone. Fighting PTSD and demons that he can't explain has left him tired and changed from the man he was before he went overseas.

The only thing he feels like he excels at anymore is being a criminal, and he gladly does it for his brothers of the Heaven Hill MC. The only people who took him in when no one else knew what to make of his anger and frustration.

When Jessica arrives, however, she's a trigger for everything he's trying to forget. She makes him remember who he was before his life went to hell; she makes him want to get himself back. While working through those issues, he and Jessica are racing against an unknown enemy.

As they both work to trust each other and figure out just who her enemies are, they learn that love is never easy. They have to decide if the victory is worth the battle.

Dirty Little Secret
(Fifth in the Heaven Hill Series)

Sister
Lone survivor
Scared, but tough

Christine Stone has lived through a lot since the day she was born. Her older brother left her without a backwards glance, leaving her with parents who wanted to use her to better themselves in their cult-like religious sect.

Days after legally becoming an adult, she's given to an older man for an arranged marriage that will change her life forever. Escape is the only way her life can be saved. When she succeeds and sets out to make a new life for herself, she meets Travis Steele—communications and security officer for the Heaven Hill MC.

Loner
Protector of secrets
Level-headed and steady

Travis Steele has been on the periphery of the Heaven Hill MC for a long time. Quiet, he takes his job seriously. He is the protector of the group, in charge with keeping family and friends safe.

When one meeting with the sister of his friend turns into more, he struggles with where to draw the line. She needs a friend, and Travis prides himself in being what other people need, often sacrificing himself for others. As he discovers the life that Christine has been forced to live, it opens up old wounds, new wounds, and secrets that everyone thought long buried.

Turning a chance meeting into love is hard, especially when everyone has a dirty little secret.

31398446R00140

Made in the USA
Charleston, SC
16 July 2014